IF YOU FAIL TO DREAM. ALL YOU HAVE LEFT ARE NIGHTMARES

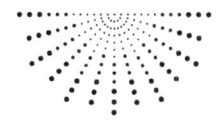

SIMON THORPE

CONTENTS

1. Thursday 22/11/2018	1
2. Tuesday 23/8/1485 (Julian Calendar)	17
3. Saturday 24th November 2018	31
4. December 1485	46
5. Sunday 24/11/2018	62
6. Monday 23/2/1501	79
7. Wednesday Morning 23/11/2018	96
8. Monday 19 April 1918	112
9. Wednesday afternoon 23/11/2018	128
10. Wednesday 28/11/1918	148
11. Wednesday Evening 28/11/2018	164
12. Wednesday 5th December 2018	179
13. Thursday 24th November 2018	191
14. Thursday 11.00 am 24/11/2018	209
15. Thursday afternoon 24/11/2018	224
16. Thursday 2.30pm 24/11/2018	239
Epilogue	251

1
THURSDAY 22/11/2018

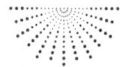

'A mother's arms are more comforting than anyone else's.'—
Princess Diana

'Rab, RAB!' Opening the kitchen door, the middle-aged woman took one quick step out into the tiny hallway and really bellowed.

'RAB – the bloody taxi will be here in five minutes, get your arse out of bed and down here NOW.'

Pulling at her bedraggled hair with one hand she tugged her loose and shabby dressing gown tight around her body with the other and went back to the kitchen table. She sat a little too quickly. The small and rickety chair appeared to struggle with the initial impact, but it did settle. Picking up the half-smoked cigarette, she took a deep drag and let out a world-weary sigh.

The plastic-topped table was festooned with her makeup, lipsticks and other parts of her 'war paint', and she was going to do battle that day!

Hearing Rab open his bedroom door she forced a smile onto her lips.

'Rab, Rab – come here darling, quickly.'

Her son appeared in the doorway. He was wearing an ill-fitting school shirt that hadn't been washed for some time. It held the motif of a rising sun on it and he had a baseball cap perched over his thick curly hair. His face usually carried a deep scowl but he looked hopeful at the sound of his mother.

She stood up and moved towards him, softly taking an ear in each of her hands.

'Darling, listen, I don't need any phone calls from school today, especially between eleven and twelve.'

She twisted each ear and repeated with emphasis, 'I cannot lose this customer, not if you want to eat.'

Rab grimaced with pain and allowed his head to be moved up and down as if agreeing. She noticed that he smelt quite badly that morning and couldn't bring herself to give him a kiss. Instead, she turned away and said over her shoulder, 'have some toast or somink and try to be good.'

With that they both heard a car toot.

'Mum.'

She had returned back to the chair and reconvened applying her eye shadow. She didn't respond to him and he turned away, opening the door and shouted out

'You're a, a'—he struggled to say the word, and, pausing for effect, shouted out—'A WHORE.'

Running out towards the waiting taxi, he felt a tear drop trickle down his cheek and he angrily wiped it away. The driver knew better than to open the door or make small talk.

Rab threw himself inside on the back seat and the taxi started up.

Within ten minutes it pulled up outside the Peabody Estate. A sprawling mix of traditional council flats and maisonettes. The place looked as run down as it was, children seemed to be everywhere. Their mothers predominantly large, wearing a loose top and tight leggings, their hair pulled up to the 'Croydon Facelift'. There was a lot of noise, with the women often shouting at the children hanging around a pushchair or being too engrossed on their phones to really notice what was going on. There were eight blocks of flats that surrounded one open space with a fenced off concreted area boasting some tatty swings and a slide. It was the type of place that noticed strangers but didn't care about anyone that actually lived there. Rab idly looked out of the car window and traced the balconies along the walkways with his eye. The doors of the flats were coloured in sequence: red, yellow, green. It seemed to hypnotise him.

The taxi driver, Asif, pulled up outside one of the tower blocks and stopped the engine. Rab had calmed down, the therapy of the colours had done its usual trick. But there was still the rage that was always part of him. He wanted to fight someone, to hit and to hurt, but instead, he too, waited. This routine was repeated every day. They waited for precisely three minutes. Both of them knew that Tom wouldn't appear, he hadn't now for two months. But the taxi had to try to collect him every day and would lose the contract with the Local Authority if there was no effort.

The next stop was for H. H was a year older than Rab and in Year 10, but his fifteenth birthday was still some way off. He talked too much in Rab's opinion but he could be relied upon to have some 'fags'. H clambered in and lumbered down into the seat next to Rab. Quietly, Rab felt the half a Rizla being passed to him as H was talking about the latest car he would like. No one ever listened to H and no one knew what his full name was. With H you just had to relax and let him pour out his 'verbal diarrhoea' as Rab would say. Rab fingered the self-made cigarette with satisfaction.

The taxi collected one other boy. He was the youngest to be picked up and was wisely scared of saying a word. The boys had a hierarchy and anyone testing it would suffer the consequences. The boy had learnt the hard way about letting H rattle on, having once laughed and joked about the constant barrage of words, the resulting smack had hurt. He sat in the front as usual, the bigger boys lorded it in the back.

Asif looked in his mirror and could see that Rab seemed even more angry than usual. Rab's eyes were truly terrifying and Asif wondered, not for the first time, just what it was like to work at their school.

The driver had made good time that morning and turned into a lay-by he had used before. Rab and H smiled as the car pulled to a halt and they both clambered out.

'Sweet mate, sweet,' said H and accepted the lighter off Asif, who proffered it without a second thought. H and Rab lit up and were soon relaxing as they passed the rolled-up cigarette between themselves. They still ignored the boy in the front, who had kept his head low and deliberately did not look at the older boys.

'Did ya bring them?' asked Rab.

H nodded and gave a wide grin.

'No sweat my man, no sweat.' He then flicked his fingers and made a clicking noise which he hoped made him appear 'West Indian'.

'No, Rasclad, no.' Rab gave him a dismissive look. He hated white kids trying to appear as though they were black.

H gave a sheepish smile revealing teeth that had been badly neglected. But he held out a blister pack of tablets, their blue hue just visible through the plastic covering.

Both boys couldn't contain their good humour and their 'high five' was instinctive and as good a gesture of friendship as either would ever allow to be seen.

The taxi soon joined the tailback of ten other cars/people carriers as they moved slowly up the drive and towards the school. Rab could see the large building come into view and part of his anger abated as he actually looked forward to arriving. He didn't know that the main front was actually built in the sixteenth century nor that it had been used as a hospital during the first World War, but he did know that the school had been having boys with behavioural and social difficulties for some years as he had completed a piece of artwork explaining this which had been placed in the front entrance. He really hoped that he had Art that day. He was very creative and found the opportunity to be practical really soothing; he always got the best grades for Art and, of course, from Mr Smith, or 'Smithy' as the boys called him.

As he and H got out of the taxi one of the staff, a Ms Arnold, shouted out, with an amazing level of cheerfulness, 'Good morning, Rab, and Hi to Harry and H—'

Before she could finish her early-morning greeting, H had started to talk, well, he had never really stopped in the car. He gushed, 'Hiya Darling, hope you didn't miss me too much?'

Ms Arnold, as she insisted on being called, gave an easy smile and tutted aloud.

'H, behave today and perhaps I might sit with you at lunch.' She then fussed through the questions she had to ask, checking about lunch arrangements and the choices they might want for break-time activities. Everybody had to be accounted for after they had eaten lunch and there was a good range of choices available for both food and things to do.

As they finished fielding her questions she turned to go to another taxi and greeted those arrivals, but, surreptitiously, she spoke quietly under her breath to Rab.

'Rab, I've got a clean school shirt if you'd like to borrow it?'

Rab glanced round worried that someone else might have heard, but everyone was out of earshot. He nodded his appreciation but held his haughty expression.

She gave a brief smile and nodded back. He knew that when the bell went he would hang back and be able to swap the shirt without anyone knowing. He cared about his appearance and hated that the clothes he had to wear were dirty. Ms Arnold was another of his 'favourites'.

He moved off towards the Multiple Use Gym Area or MUGA as it was called and quickly slipped through its tiny entrance and joined the other boys.

'Right Rab,' shouted Mr Carlyle. 'You are kicking down and on my side. 'And with that he passed the ball to Rab who instinctively flicked it up and dribbled it round one of the lads on the other side. He accelerated past with obvious skill and bore down on the goal. For a few seconds his anger at everyone and his own self-loathing were forgotten. He was where he felt safe.

At ten thirty, H and Rab met in the main foyer. The first two lessons had been hard for them as they knew they had to get good grades to be able to leave as soon as break started. The school only had seventy-five boys, all of whom had been taxied in from all over the County. It had been remarked by one East Sussex official that 'it was easier getting into Eton than St Thomas's. But Rab was only interested in one lad today. When the much younger Tel swaggered into view Rab gave H the briefest of nods. Tel was just twelve years old and already making himself known as a very likely lad in the school. He had been in lots of restraints already and it had taken more staff than usual to hold him down and placate him. Tel also had a 'credit card' scar across his mouth and was perversely proud of it.

He caught sight of Rab and quickly glanced over his shoulder. There was just the usual bustle of boys heading for either the MUGA or the safety of the computer room. There was an unwritten rule that staff would not appear for two or three minutes allowing the 'smokers' to have their fix without being caught. Tel gave an imperceptible nod and the three of them left the building and huddled together just round a convenient corner.

H started speaking at once, his words rushing forth as a gush of expletives. 'You know what I means'. He finished off with, 'here is the gear, you take half and give us the other half at the end of the day,' proffering the blister pack of red tablets to Tel.

The young pupil smiled, his young face looking older than his years. His role in his class of seven other boys was self-appointed leader and he knew that they would buy the tablets if he gave it his approval.

'nah H, I take half and two freebies...'

Tel wasn't able to finish his sentence. Rab had moved quickly and with deadly intent. He hoisted the younger boy off his feet and against the wall.

Tel's eyes revealed real fear, he had seen what Rab was capable of and even though the local gang had split his mouth open, leaving his 'tell-tale' scar, it had been controlled violence. No one knew when Rab would ever stop once he had got started.

Rab glowered, his strong hands holding the blue school jumper firmly and he bent his mouth lower, so as to whisper into Tel's ear.

'Don't get greedy, and never try to negotiate, capeesh?'

Rab wasn't sure what 'capeesh' meant, but he had heard it being used in a gangster film and had stored it up ready for the right occasion. He then let the boy down. H had been checking that the coast was clear. He surreptitiously dropped the blister pack into Tel's pocket. The deal had been done.

At 10.45 the boys started to wander back into the school. The front of which had a large facade, the crumbling brick-work at odds with the new block that was linked onto it. H gave a quick thumbs up to Rab and went right past the Art room. Rab loitered and tentatively poked his head through the door.

'Smithy?' He called out and gave an involuntary smile as the large figure of the teacher emerged from his stock room.

'Good morning to you young Rab,' he boomed out. It was generally agreed that Mr Smith only had one volume, and that was loud, very loud. His large physique was dominated with a massive protruding stomach. The rumour was that he had once been a useful prop forward, but the muscle he had once been able to boast about was turning to fat quicker than he had hoped.

'What can I do for you today Buddy, come to check how it's dried eh?'

Rab nodded, his apprehension heightened by the prospect of seeing his latest project nearly completed. He had made a clay effigy of an old image that projected out of part of a wall near the top of the driveway. Smithy had explained that it was part of an old heraldic shield and the creature was called a griffin. The idea of a lion's body having an eagle's head had fascinated him and he had wanted to make a clay image of it. He was so pleased when Smithy pulled back a dusty sheet and Rab saw his work.

'All it needs now is painting.' The Teacher looked very pleased with it and beamed at Rab.

Rab gently laid a finger on his work and hurried off to his English lesson. He felt proud and that was an emotion he had rarely known.

An hour later and just as Rab had started to write an answer to a question that he felt was really silly he saw the Head of Care, Mr Evans, talking quietly to Mr Green just outside the classroom. Rab saw one of them look at him and then talk into his Walkie Talkie. Rab felt a flush of anger ripple through his body. He hated both of them and knew that something was up.

A few minutes later Ms Arnold appeared. She looked through the glass part of the door, made eye contact with Rab and quickly looked away. Rab knew with a certainty that something had happened, but surely Tel hadn't 'coughed' he thought to himself? There were only four other boys in Rab's class that day and the fact that those two men plus Ms Arnold were outside made it nearly absolute that they expected trouble, and from him.

Mr Evans opened the door and said, 'Excuse me Mrs Miller, could we have a quick word with Rab please?' He then looked directly at Rab and gestured with his head for the boy to come out into the corridor.

'No way,' Rab stood up, pushing the table away from him and onto the floor. He felt the blood rush through his body and his face was quickly flushed.

'What you want, you say here and now.'

Rab glanced up and saw that the time was 11.30. He felt his stomach lurch and his whole body stiffen. Everything seemed distorted and livid. His head was thumping and his hands were clenched into fists.

'Calm Rab, just come outside please, no one needs to know all your business now.' Mr Evans opened the door fully and stepped away from the entrance. Rab could see Ms Arnold smiling at him, imploring him to comply.

Rab reluctantly started to go towards the door and he heard Mr Green say, ever so quietly, 'I've asked the office to ring his mother,' to Ms Arnold.

Ten minutes later the three staff were still struggling to hold Rab on the floor. Someone had split their lip and the class had been evacuated to another room. Rab was incoherent in his swearing and the adrenalin rush meant that the two large men were unable to contain him.

Through the red fog that dominated his mind he could hear a distant voice.

'Rab, calm down, it's OK, calm.'

Ms Arnold was holding his hand, he became aware that someone had his legs, he thought they might be sitting on them. His head was pushed down on the floor and to the left. They always did that, so as to avoid being spat on. His right arm was spread out wide and someone was holding it very firmly. He was in pain and he tried to focus on the voice.

'Rab, we want to let go of you, but we need to trust you, so we will do it in stages, can you hear me?'

Rab tried to nod but his head was pinioned and he struggled to say 'Get off me. GEDDOFFME.'

'Rab, you've been spitting at us and trying to hit out, we need to stop this, if we get off your legs will you not move?'

Rab could feel the tears pricking his eyes. He wanted it to stop. He wanted everything to stop.

He quietly said 'yes' and felt the pressure release from his legs. He lay prone whilst the man that had his arm and head then released his grasp. Rab knew the routine and he just lay still. He could feel Ms Arnold holding his hand and he moved his finger to acknowledge her.

Mr Evans then said 'Rab, can you get up and sit on this chair please?'

Rab looked up and saw that someone had placed a chair in the corridor and he quickly hauled himself up and sat on it, he kept his head low so that no one could see his tears. They were not tears of pain and no longer of anger, but of humiliation.

'Have you rung my mum?' he asked. 'Please say that you haven't?'

He didn't want to sound plaintive but he was remembering what his mother had said.

A fresh round of tears poured from him and he felt a deep despair. A kind of hollowness that he doubted would ever be filled.

The two men slowly got to their feet. Both looked quite shaken and Mr Green started to tentatively stretch his back out. Ms Arnold came over to the chair and went down on her haunches. She took his hand again and gave him an encouraging smile.

'Well done Rab, you came out of that really quickly, well done.'

Rab turned a tearful eye towards her, taking in her earnestness and generosity. He hated the two men but not her. Even though she had been part of the Restraint too.

Mr Green started to speak, to explain that the 'Positive handling' incident had been necessary and that no one had wanted to hurt him. Rab had heard it all before and knew that this litany had to be said and recorded. He didn't care and repeated his question.

'Have you rung my mum yet?'

Mr Evans nodded and moved quickly as Rab exploded again. This time both men were thrown around the corridor and Ms Arnold grimaced as she saw them upend Rab to the floor and hold him with even more intensity than before. Not for the first time she struggled with the terminology 'positive handling.'

An hour later, Rab's Mother emerged from her taxi. She wobbled on her high heels and her tight skirt hindered her journey from the car to the front entrance.

She looked furious and brushed aside Mr Evans handshake.

'Where is the little bleeder?' She flounced through the front door and into Mr Carlyle's office. She was anxious and hated having to come to the school, but, as ever, covered this up with being overly aggressive.

Rab jumped up as she entered but wasn't quick enough to stop the blow she successfully landed on the side of his head.

'Yer stupid idiot!' She bellowed.

'That's it, my best client and he's dropped me.' she stood in front of her son unintimidated even though he was a good three inches taller than her, even with her high heels on.

'Well, what have you got to say for yourself?'

Mr Carlyle tried to step between the mother and son but as he moved both of them turned to stare at him. Almost challenging him to intervene in a family row. The headteacher took in how pale her complexion was and her bare right arm was laced with small scars and pinpricks.

Mrs Jerome turned her whole body to face the headteacher. Her voice is thick with sarcasm.

'Send a taxi for me and just reckon I'll get it in?' She turned her face, caked with cheap makeup and heavy mascara, up towards him.

'Just like I'm some lackey that has to do what you say?' She paused whilst she had a quick calculation and then poured out her criticisms.

'I thought this school was meant to cope with boys like my Rab? Yet all I get is phone calls and then you just exclude him. Well, I've had enough, you can keep him, or get the Social to take him away. Useless sod is no good to me.' She paused for breath and then seemed to crumple. She looked around herself and sat down. The moment was too much and her tears started to flood down her face. Two black lines streaming down her face soon smeared over her cheeks and her hands were grasping each other.

Mr Carlyle quickly realised that bringing her here had been a mistake. He looked at Rab, who had sat down and was staring into his own hands, his anger abated and a sinister stillness hung over him. His face was slightly red from her blow, his shirt stained with his sweat.

After a very difficult fifteen minutes, Mrs Jerome had left the school, alone. The agreed sanction had been a removal of what points Rab had scored that week plus isolation for two days. Mr Carlyle gave a brief smile as he saw the taxi leave the drive and barked out his instructions to Mr Evans.

Ordinarily such a serious restraint would have resulted in a fixed term exclusion. But, on this occasion, he understood why Rab had reacted as he did and felt a degree of sympathy for him. The whole situation could have been handled so much better. He talked through his decision with the staff that had been involved and ensured that the Positive Handling form had been completed. Fortunately, the staff had agreed with his actions.

Rab walked slowly up the drive towards the small building, he was looking forward to having some time away from the other boys and there might even be an opportunity for him to learn more about griffins. Having Ms Arnold with him made the punishment almost a pleasure.

They entered the outhouse and she pushed open the large interior door.

'Right Rab, this is home for two days, so get used to it,' she said cheerfully. She opened the folder she had brought with her and set out his work pens and other stationary.

'You've got me until the end of the day, so no slacking'.

Rab sat down as directed and felt pleased with the outcome. He wasn't excluded and had Ms Arnold to himself for two hours. They had eaten with the other boys at lunchtime and Rab had managed to give Tel a look that said 'we will have words later, but you had better start worrying'. He felt sure that it had been the young boy who had 'told' about the drugs.

Ms Arnold had explained that all the boys in Tel's class had been sick and complained of a bad headache. Tel had sold the tablets too quickly and cheaply, he had then panicked and blurted out where he had got them once Mr Carlyle had threatened him with the police.

It was only when H had explained that the tablets were only migraine ones that he had pinched from his granny that there hadn't been more serious punishments. Ms Arnold had laughed at the prospect of all the Year Seven boys being ill through the night, one of the side effects was bad diarrhoea. She had an odd sense of humour on occasion.

Rab settled down to his work and only glanced up when one of his sheets had been completed.

He gave a gasp as he saw one of the claws of the griffin. He looked carefully at the ceiling and pointed upwards.

'Look Miss, there's 'undreds of 'em'.

2
TUESDAY 23/8/1485 (JULIAN CALENDAR)

The word 'anchoress' – most were women – comes from a Greek word, anachoreo, meaning 'to withdraw or retire'. - **The Times 1985**

St Haura Village 1485.

The powerful shire horse shuddered to a halt as the metal-clad knight pulled hard at the reins. A shield was tossed down, embedding itself into the soft soil. The heraldic griffin emblazoned on it appeared to bristle at the impact. The knight lumbered off the thankful horse and looked around him. Seeing the priest cowering nearby he shouted.

'You, priest, tell me where Lady Mary is if you value your ears.' His roar seemed to physically grasp the cleric and his body.

'Lord, she is within her church.' The priest clutched at the cross that hung around his chest. A look of fear justly etched upon his face.

'No,' bellowed the Knight. He looked around him and then grabbed at the priest. His gauntlet cut the priest's face in the process.

He swung him high in the air and onto the floor, deftly pinioning him to the ground with his shield which he had retrieved, the griffin image painted on it the only thing that the priest could see.

'What say you, her church, I can only see this Manor House.' He corrected himself. 'My Manor House.'

The Knight, Sir Richard of Holme, having been only recently raised to that rank but a day ago, was spitting in his anger and frustration and barely heard his steward speaking to him, nor felt the gentle tug on his arm.

'Sire, the priest may die and we will all be sent to hell and damnation. Leave the pitiful creature and will find the Lady.'

Sir Richard glanced up and saw that his steward had already secured his horse, tethered to a nearby tree. He released his hold of the priest and stood upright, his shield in one hand, the other pointing down. His excitement at returning back to Haura and the adrenalin that had coursed through his veins during the heat of the recent battle had made him both impatient and impetuous.

'What's your name man and where is this church?'

The priest slowly stood to his full height which was substantially shorter than the impressive stature of the knight before him.

'Father Thomas Sire.' He spoke in a faltering way and made sure that he kept his eyes downcast. The temper of Richard was very well known in these parts.

'I live in St Haura village, I'm the son of Peter, one of your tenant farmers.'

Sir Richard gave a hush guffaw and turned to his Steward.

'Do you know this wreck of a man, or Peter, his father?'

The steward, an older man with an old scar that ran down one side of his face gave a mirthless smile and shook his head. Neither man had any patience with the church but he, rather than his master, was more aware of the possible repercussions if there was any foolhardy act.

The Manor House that stood away from them was mostly made of stone and had the unusual luxury of a second story. The wings were a mixture of wood and thatch and it passed for a semblance of wealth in those days. But had seen better days and had a dilapidated feel about it.

The priest held a trembling hand up and gestured up and away from the House, he gulped deeply and said, in a rush 'St Haura is now St Mary's Church, by order of the Bishop.'

The priest appeared exhausted by the effort of speaking and felt an urge to make a sign of the cross. He sincerely believed that he had spoken his last words.

The knight raised his arm and casually brushed the priest aside and strode towards the large wooden door of the House, he raised his fist and banged loudly. He had heard the priest but had not fully understood what had been meant. He had dreamt of this moment for so long and intended to drive through his intentions.

'Let me in, a leech upon your souls – I demand entrance.'

Sir Richard hammered at the door with an increasing intensity. He knew of no other strategy but to use his might and always expected that this would win through. After several powerful blows the door began to open, as soon as there was a big enough crack he forced the end of his sword through and pulled it open fully. Lady Mary's father stood in the entrance. He cowered and struggled to look the knight in his eye.

The strength of the older man had gone. The once strong shoulders now sagged and his eyes were ringed with black through a lack of sleep whilst red with too much wine. But he still managed to croak out 'So, it is you, I expected nothing else but.' he paused and seemed to dig deep from within himself.

'You are too late, the deed is done. She is in her church now.'

Sir Richard barged past the man and into the Manor House fully and, with his sword held out in front of him, glanced around the hall, so familiar to him and yet now feeling strange and sinister. Turning back towards the old man he said,

'You, you, and, and that priest talk of a church, yet all I see is this house,' he gave a smile of pleasure before concluding, 'my house now.'

He raised his shield once more and brought it down with a crack onto the poorly-tiled floor. The end became embedded and the griffin, bright with its eyes appearing to glow in the light cast by the fire that burnt in the fireplace, seemed to claw at the air. The manor was not large and its main hall was the principal meeting place. The large wooden table and fire usually dominated the hall. But it was dark now, the cost too much for it to rage all day as it once had done. and the fire was the critical source of light. The old man stared at the shield in dismay, his sadness and sense of surrender galvanising the knight even more. Sir Richard appeared to gather his composure.

'I have come to claim my right. The Lady Mary will be wed to me before autumn comes. Our new king has agreed. Richard could not help but sneer as he finished his sentence.

Sir John's mouth gaped open, he had heard that Richard the Third was going to face the upstart Henry Tudor at Bosworth field but hadn't realised that Henry had won and was now proclaiming himself the new king. His shoulders slumped even more and he wondered that if the Plantagenet House was extinguished what hope was there for him and his family?

He felt that his life was swimming away, beyond his reach. He looked up and tried to connect with the young man before him.

'Richard, Richard, I know we've fallen out but believe me, Lady Mary is already Sister Mary and lives within her church.' He stopped and pointed out of the door and towards the tiny building that sat at the top of the path that led to the house.

'She is now a nun,' he stopped to think of the right word. He looked up and said 'an Anchorite Nun.'

With one blow Sir Edward fell to the floor, his head crashing onto the crudely tiled floor. Sir Richard gasped and he looked at his fist; he was prepared to strike another blow but saw the blood oozing from the old man's skull. Death had already arrived for him.

Sir Richard raised his head and gave a sardonic grin. He felt omnipotent right now. With the death of King Edward and then the news of his sons being murdered in the tower, undoubtedly by the hand of that fiend Richard the Third, he had backed everything on supporting Henry Tudor.

He had gambled everything and now was victorious. He stood in the hall and raised both his hands aloft crying out.

'You fool John, I have your house, I have your griffin and I swear I will marry your daughter too.'

His Steward rushed over to the prostrate lord of the manor and crouched over him.

'He is dead my Lord.' Tom, the Steward, looked up, he was holding a chain in his hand.

'Lord, Lord, what is this?'

Sir Richard rushed over and grasping the chain gave a wrench and held his prize aloft. It was a small gold talon. The token of the family and a symbol of the griffin. He threw back his head and gave a loud shriek of joy. His support of Henry Tudor at the Battle of Bosworth Field made him safe from possible reprisal and he meant to take all that he could.

Mary was busy supervising the additional wall being hurriedly created next to the outbuilding. Two local masons were working hard and both kept glancing warily around them as they laboured.

'Fear not Master Simon, there's time yet,' she lied.

She knew that it was likely Richard would arrive very soon. His long-held desire to marry her had brought her whole family to its knees. Richard had been buying up nearby land over the past two years and he had been, slowly and methodically, accruing their debts from the local Jews. At the time of

Edward IV's death in 1483 the once proud Griffin family had become little more than the Manor House in which they lived and their few tenant farmers impoverished through lack of care from her father.

She clutched at the locket around her neck and, again, nervously looked behind her. The adapted building now looked more like a church. It had always served as a small chapel for her family and some of the villagers, those dedicated enough to make the two-mile journey from Haura. The few gravestones dotted around it clearly signposted its religious status but the very small, short steeple and transept now looked at odds with the hastily constructed annex that was fixed to the east part.

Holding her sodden woollen skirts, she ducked through the remaining gap and looked around her new surroundings.

'My Lady, are you sure about this?' The large Mason had also ducked his head down and was looking at her, blocking out the little light that had been streaming in.

She clutched her locket once more and nodded her assent. She hadn't had time to don the clothes of a nun, nor had she cut her long plait, but she felt confident that once she was housed within the confines of the church she would be safe. The image of being incarcerated within this tiny space hadn't really dominated her thoughts, just the need to have constructed it.

The Mason grunted something indecipherable to his apprentices and they bent low and quickly filled in the space with their bricks, making it complete with mortar, the smell of which filled the small space.

Mary faced the wall of the church and pulled aside the small curtain that covered part of it. Behind it was a space no more than two feet long and one foot wide. She leant forward and was able to punch most of her face through the gap and thus was able to see most of the church.

She saw the far wall covered with the story of Samson and Delilah and had a rush of a memory of her as a small child helping paint the images with her boyhood friend, Robin. Robin, with his laughing eyes and ready smile. Was he really dead, slain at Bosworth Field?

She felt her face become wet with tears and she craned her neck further to look towards the Chancel. She couldn't see the Font properly but was able to hear her servant talking.

'Beth, Beth, come here,' She called out firmly and heard the swish of Beth's skirts as the small older woman came into view. Beth gave a gasp and looked horrified.

'My Lady, are you in? Is it done?'

Mary gave an enthusiastic grin, her sadness dissipated at the sight of her servant and the success of her venture so far. She was now part of the tiny church, she was an anchorite nun. Or so she believed.

Sir Richard spurred his horse up the small hill. His anger knew no bounds and the sight of the outhouse building only hardened his resolve. He would not allow such a foolish thing. Mary would be his wife and the griffin pennant would fly over his Manor House. He slowed his giant horse down and had a quick image of the bricks being pulled down.

. . .

The idiots back at the Manor House were forgotten and the death of Sir Edward didn't register on his very low moral compass. All his thoughts were on Mary. He slowed to a trot and bellowed out,

'You there, Master Mason! Stop this nonsense at once.'

The Mason stood to his full height. His powerful arms made muscular by years of hard work shifting and shaping large stones hung limply at his sides. He was aware of Sir Richard's temper and how quickly the knight's longsword would slice through his body.

After just a second thought he bowed his head and said a short prayer. He felt the horse's breath on his head and heard the clunk of heavy armour as the knight dismounted.

'Well Mason, I can see only this small wall, what is this nonsense?' Sir Robert moved past the mason and up to the recently constructed wall, its mortar still glistening wet and then he noticed the small space, about two small bricks high and three across. Imperiously he thrust part of his face through it.

'What's this space for? Why, I can see through.' And then he heard a shuffling from the corner.

'What's this again you vagabond, show yourself,' he bellowed and craned his head so as to see who was making the noise.

The look of horror on his face and one of extreme incredulity could only be seen by Mary as she stood to her full height and looked up to him. His nose and clear blue eyes were hardly visible as he blocked out the restricted sunlight.

She bent low and scooped up a candle, holding it between her teeth she adeptly struck the two bits of flint gaining enough spark to light the protruding wick.

The newly lit up small room showed it to be only four foot wide and eight foot long at best. The rough pile of hay in one corner and a small desk and chair were its only furniture. She slowly moved the candle round in an arc and said 'behold my new home Richard, you've taken my real one and welcome you to it. I want nothing to do with you anymore. I'll live and die here.'

Richard bent his head and tried to punch against the newly constructed wall, but he was too constricted to gain enough purchase. He gave a cry of anguish and attempted to put his arm through but his head filled the small space.

He could see the look of triumph on her face and withdrew his head. Words failed him as he realised the extent of her denial of him and how brutal she was prepared to be so as to thwart him. All the dreams he'd ever had as a boy. His plans and schemes over the years and the huge expectation he'd enjoyed when standing on the bloody battlefield of Bosworth. Were they all to come to nought?

Richard slumped onto the floor, his armour making a clanging noise and he sat wearily.

'Sire, Sire, what ails you?' Cried his steward, only recently arriving at the small chapel.

'Is this what the priest had meant? Is this the newly consecrated church?'

He shuddered back when he heard Mary cry out in a voice bordering on the hysterical.

'It is, it is. This is now the Church of St Thomas's and I live within it.' The steward looked towards the sound and saw her face looking out. Her eyes held a manic gleam and she cried out again.

'Come not back here again Richard nor you Steward Godfrey. I'll have no more to do with you, but, hark my words. The griffin will die with me'.

Sir Richard looked at the steward as he sat. His shoulders curled and the energy had drained from him. The steward hurried across and bent to help him up. The spittle from her lips landed on his cheek as he righted himself and he quickly half carried the large man away. He turned his back on the now screaming young woman from within her self-imposed incarceration.

Sir Richard whispered to Godfrey,

'All that I've done is for naught. I'm too late to hold her hand in marriage. This day she has…' he gulped and the steward had to bend his head even lower to hear what Sir Richard was going to say. he had never seen his master like this. All the anger of his self-righteous sense of belief had disappeared.

'…Become a Nun.'

The two soldiers staggered a good fifty yards before Richard was lowered onto a raised stone. Both were panting and the steward asked 'What mean you Sire, how can she be a nun? It makes no sense'

Richard gave a desperate shake of his large head. His plans lay in tatters now and he had believed that he had gained all that he had ever wanted, the rank and lands of a wealthy knight. But, what he had always wanted, more than anything else, was the hand of Mary in marriage.

'She now lives within that church, it is her convent and she lives alone. I can never enter that, not even I.' Richard gave one last gasp.

'I will never have her.'

The steward sat with his knight for a while. The cackling laughter of the young woman could still be heard and Godfrey wondered if she had gone mad. Surely only someone who has lost their senses would do such a thing?

Godfrey went and retrieved the great steed and helped his Lord up and onto the horse. They needed to be anywhere but here.

Richard rode back to the Manor House and saw that the door was still open. Dismounting his horse he saw that the threshold was blood soaked and he heard two sergeant at arms who were hovering over the slain Sir John. They looked up and were crestfallen at the sight of the knight and his steward. Both Richard and Godfrey looked battle hardened and their grim faces showed that they would give no quarter to any difficulties. Whereas the two sergeants were soldiers in name only.

'You there,' the steward let go of Sir Richards horse and took command of the situation.

'Sir Edward here was killed as he refused to acknowledge the new king, King Henry the Seventh.'

Godfrey gave a loud whoop and cry shouting out 'I say hail the new king, King Henry the Seventh, what say you?'

The servant who had loyally served Sir Edward for twenty years and had known Sir Richard when he was merely a ward immediately sang out 'Hail King Henry.'

The younger servant, who was a little slow in his thinking, quickly followed the example of the older man.

Sir Richard seemed to awake from his reverie.

'Well said men.' He looked up and seemed to grow. Then, shouting out, he declared 'well said.'

He went on.

'I declare that, even though this man died a traitor to the true king, let him be buried with all due pomp and ceremony at the family burial ground.'

The knight had stood tall and was back to his full stature, and his voice carried true resonance as he declared 'The king, King Henry the Seventh himself has stated that these lands are now mine in name and by right. Let no man declare otherwise or else he will have to answer to me.' As he finished his short speech he raised his sword above his head and held his stance.

There were only three men that saw this, yet word of it spread through the village and across the enclosed fields and valleys that encompassed his lands.

Father Thomas was sent for and the dead body was raised gently and laid out in the Manor House. Within a few hours there could be seen a steady trickle of croft holders that came up to the house to declare their allegiance to Sir Richard and to affirm that Henry was the true king. Anyone that held a house of at least two or three rooms had to attend and many that were held in fealty to them. Even the women came, their long dresses and chemises dirty from the long hours that they toiled, both in their cottages and at home.

By the end of August all of Richard's domain was established and whilst everyone had to pass by the small chapel as they made their way to the large house, few stopped to talk to the woman who stared at them from the small glassless window that faced out of the newly built wall.

Mary settled down to life as best she could in her self-induced cell, safe within the confines of the small chapel.

3
SATURDAY 24TH NOVEMBER 2018

'I have absolutely no pleasure in the stimulants in which I sometimes so madly indulge. It has not been in the pursuit of pleasure that I have periled life and reputation and reason. It has been the desperate attempt to escape from torturing memories, from a sense of insupportable loneliness and a dread of some strange impending doom.'—**Edgar Allen Poe.**

Rab moved along the orange plastic-coated bench until he could go no further. He wanted to pull his hood up and over his head but realised that this might be frowned on and merely bowed his neck. His fingers had an urge to pull his mobile phone out of his pocket and it seemed odd not to be staring at its cracked and dirty screen.

Warily he glanced to his left when he heard a noise and saw an old woman shuffle along halfway on the bench before him. She was on the lower one and did little to obscure his line of sight.

'COURT RISE,' bellowed the Usher and Rab stood up quickly. He looked forward and thus downwards as the public gallery was perched up high. He saw the two magistrates stride into the court. One stood behind the middle chair and waited for his colleague to arrive, positioning himself on his wing.

The middle magistrate waited, as though for dramatic effect and bowed his head saying 'Good morning please sit.'

Everyone else then sat and Rab was now able to take stock of the whole courtroom. The old woman had been slow to stand and now took her time to settle. Rab felt the eyes of the magistrates gravitate upwards and they appeared to study her intently.

The one in the middle bent low and said something to his colleague, listened and nodded. They both appeared to smile. Rab was confused as to who was who before him and whilst he had been in trouble with the law on numerous occasions, he had always avoided actually being taken to court.

Just in front of the two magistrates and lower than them sat a woman who already looked overburdened and busy. Her long desk was strewn with papers and she appeared half hidden by the computer screen in front of her.

'Your Worships, we have a full list today and may the court start with case of Jessica Higgins.'

As soon as she had sad this someone stood up and faced the JPs, he set out the case and the day had begun in earnest.

After a couple of hours Rab had worked out who was who and had been transfixed by the proceedings. It was the only court sitting on a Saturday morning and most of the defendants had been remanded in custody overnight. The magistrates seemed to deal with them all by either sentencing if possible or fixing a date for further trial, some were remanded in custody and the reasons for that explained. For one quite serious case whereby a transgender person had been caught with a knife crime there had been deliberations about whether they could be kept in a male prison or not.

The usher was the one that Rab found most amusing, as she wore a long black gown and fussed about but actually doing very little. The old woman had left after seeing her son remanded in custody. He had visited his ex-wife so as to see his children and had breached a restraining order. Rab had started to think that his trip to Brighton had been a waste of time, even though it had interested him.

Then he heard the heavy thud of the three men behind him. He half turned to see who they were and quickly jerked his head back, staring fixedly ahead away from them. All three were heavily muscled with extravagant tattoos festooning their arms and necks. Rab felt the prickle of fear rise through his body and his head sprouted sweat. He had come to court as he had heard that his cousin Jason had been arrested late on Friday night. Rab had come just to report back to his aunt and mother, and he realised now why they had sent him and not themselves. The three men behind him were notorious around Moulsecoomb, people that no one messed with.

'Here he is, the little turd, 'said one.

'Yeah, he'd best keep his trap shut,' said another.

Rab kept his head low and flinched when the magistrate, or Presiding Judge as Rab had learnt, barked out 'You in the Public Gallery, please be quiet and put your phones away or I'll ask the Usher to remove them.'

Rab felt the wrath of the men behind him and wondered what that little old usher could do against the 'Blokes' as they were called when he saw two uniformed men come into the well of the court. Then, in the dock another policeman entered followed by two security guards. Rab followed the procession with a growing dread as he saw his cousin troop in and stand with his head forlornly to one side. His arm was in a sling and he was dressed in the grey jumper and tracksuit trousers which was the usual garb of anyone staying in the cells overnight. The Blokes were still behind Rab.

The CPS or, as Rab now knew them to be, Crown Prosecution Service, jumped up and started to reread aloud from his laptop. Rab heard how Jason had already been charged with human trafficking and was perceived to be a leader in the drug trade that operated in South London and had links in Brighton. The case was due to be heard in Lewes Crown Court later that month.

Rab sat and stared, his mouth had fallen open as he heard more and he was gripped in disbelief, with a strange sense of pride and utter confusion. Jason had never been very bright and, whilst he too was quite hard, he had not really been involved in any heavy-duty violence that Rab had heard about. But, then again, 'The Blokes' were here for a reason.

The prosecution had explained that when Jason Mcteer had been arrested the police had a suspicion that, during that process, he had inserted something in his rectum. They had conducted X-rays and a thorough check on all his defecations since his arrest in the belief that he had hidden a large quantity of Class A drugs.

The CPS was pausing for dramatic effect and Rab looked forward to the magistrates once more. He had realised that there were normally three of them and had surmised, accurately, that there might have been an issue getting the full quota for this Saturday.

'Your Worships, the Crown politely request that Mr Mcteer be remanded in custody until Tuesday when he will be presented to the Crown Court for the more serious charges of human trafficking. We feel that the witnesses due to be produced on that occasion would be in danger if Mr Mcteer were at large. Additionally, we request that he is remanded at Eastbourne Police Station as they have the resources to monitor his ablutions. That station has a glass toilet and if he were to pass anything they could check if it were drugs as the police suspect.'

Rab heard an inhalation of breath behind him and one of 'the Blokes' exclaim,

'I hope he can keep his cheeks together.'

Another grunted and sucked in his teeth, so audibly that Rab had an overwhelming urge to turn round.

The two magistrates moved their chairs back and huddled together for a quick debate. The Presiding Justice raised his head and declared forcibly, 'The Bench will retire to deliberate this.'

'All stand.' The usher tried to bellow out the command but it fell short. Even so, Rab scrambled to his feet. Whilst the two JPs exited the courtroom via a small door Rab felt a tap on his shoulder.

He carefully glanced round and was alarmed to find his face just inches from one of the Blokes. Rab could smell the cooked breakfast the man had enjoyed that morning and the pungent odour of a cheap deodorant.

'Who are you?' The question was emphasised with a jab into his shoulder from a sausage-sized finger. Rab stiffened and leaned back and away from any physical contact.

'He's Rab innit,' said another. 'That Pro's boy from Hastings? Yeah, she's one great...'

'Court stand!' The instruction seemed to cut through his brain and he turned back to the proceedings. The magistrates must have only gone through the door and turned around almost instantaneously.

'Please sit,' ordered the Presiding Judge and Rab obeyed. His emotions seemed to have tipped into overdrive with his anger at the jibe about his mother coupled with the fear of the Blokes and the surprise about the quick decision.

'Mr Mcteer, please remain standing.' His cousin Jason stood and after a glance up to the public gallery he turned and faced the magistrates, he bent his head slightly so as to hear through the spaces in the plastic screen that surrounded him. The two security guards also stood and one of them held a notebook and pen ready to write down what was to be said.

Rab, again, felt the total concentration of the Blokes behind him as everyone strained to hear the pronouncement. Rab just couldn't guess what was about to happen, surely his cousin wouldn't be kept in prison?

The middle magistrate looked down at his iPad and read out a carefully prepared statement. In it he explained that Rab would be remanded at Eastbourne Police station and that any bail application would not be countenanced as there was a possible threat to witnesses that would be called to his trial, due to be held at Lewes Crown Court three weeks hence.

Jason didn't have an opportunity to reply and was quickly cuffed to one of the officers and led away. The whole thing was over before anyone could react. One of the Blokes gave out a quiet whistle of disbelief and stood up. The others soon joined him.

'Shhh,' said the one that had spoken to Rab. He gestured to the others to be quiet and they solemnly made their way along the battered bench and out of the public gallery. They had, apparently, forgotten all about Rab.

Rab sat still for some minutes, he didn't pay any attention to the next case but was thinking furiously: was this good news or not? What should he tell his auntie and mum? Cautiously Rab stood up and made his way to the exit. He peered through the tiny slit of glass that ran down one side. He opened the door and stuck just his head out, there was no sign of 'The Blokes' and his escape looked safe enough.

He walked quickly down the stairs and suddenly froze. The Blokes were at the exit, apparently something had caused the alarm to be triggered and they were arguing with the guard. They stood next to the airport-style security entrance/exit. One of the security guards was looking extremely anxious, he was a portly older man and all that he had was the 'search wand'.

'ere, look, there's nuffink.' Eric, the slightly larger man pulled off his jumper and T shirt revealing his bare chest. 'I ain't stupid enough to bring summink into F'ing court am I?

The security guard quickly nodded his agreement and gave a 'thumbs up' sign to a colleague who was slowly making his way over to him. Both of them were keen for Eric and the others to be out of the court foyer and gone.

But Rab was transfixed, whilst Eric had many tattoos on his arms and even his neck, there was one that had jolted him. Across Eric's back was an intricate and multicoloured griffin. Its claws climbed up and over each shoulder and its head, that of a proud eagle, seemed to be staring at him. Its belligerence is evident.

Rab hid as best he could and waited for the furore to die away. Once he was sure that the Blokes had gone, he ventured out into James Street. It was a steep road that led down towards the pavilion. Rab followed the road and allowed his eyes to stare at the strange site that always beset him. He thought the pavilion to be a weird building and only knew about the building after an assembly that 'old Smithy' had presented to the school.

A king called George had built it to irritate his father, but it had to be only sixty miles away from London in case someone had needed to go back and run the country. It was something like that; Rab thought fondly about Smithy and wondered if he would want to hear about all the things Rab had seen and learnt from the morning.

Rab crossed the road and wandered through the grounds of the pavilion and passed the dome. Smithy had told the boys that this had been built to house the prince's horses and that there was a secret underground passage between the two buildings. Rab had laughed at the image Smithy had painted of the prince being grotesquely fat and having to hide away from the public. Rab could. Not. Believe, though, that the dome had merely been to house horses and he remembered he had shouted that out during the assembly. Rab grinned at the memory.

He then started the steep ascent up to Brighton Railway Station and passed under the bridge. There were two vagrants sitting there and one held his open palm out towards Rab.

'Nah, Bruv – I aint got nuffink.' Rab had little patience with beggars and firmly believed that people had to make their own way through life and not rely on handouts. Ironically, he did not feel that state benefits were handouts, but a right.

Rab was puffing a bit going up the steep hill and he had a flashback to the old outhouse at school where he had been in isolation last month. He smiled at the thought of Ms Arnold and recalled what she had said about the griffins he had seen on the ceiling.

He saw them in his mind's eye, surely the shape of the talon was true as on Eric's back?

His reverie was interrupted by a loud toot of a car. He spun round and saw a taxi just pulling into the rank at the station. Its driver was instantly recognisable to him. He gave Asif an uncharacteristically friendly wave. Asif wound down his window and nodded a greeting. Rab went up to the window.

Asif dropped his voice and asked 'Rab, have you got anything to sell? I might have a buyer.'

Rab was taken aback. He honestly believed that the antics he and H got up to hadn't been noticed. He also hadn't really thought about Asif being interested. But, he saw an opportunity when it appeared.

'I might have, but not 'ere innit.' Rab feigned his best scowl and made to get into the back of the taxi.

'But, if you drop me back home I'll sort you right.' He looked out of the window and saw the sky open and the rain was soon bouncing off the road. He leant back into the familiar and comfortable seat. If only life was always this easy he thought to himself and soon started to plot. It must be easy to find some coloured tablets somewhere?

∼

Two hours later he was sitting in his aunt's flat, it was only a few roads away from his own. But her flat was part of an intimidating block of twelve stories high. It arched into a semi-sphere with a fenced off concrete-based football area and he still played there most weekends. The fencing reached up to the second floor and the ball could easily be kicked onto the balcony of the flats that overlooked it. The lifts were rarely working but Rab was lucky that day, he held his breath.

Anyone who was a stranger had to have a very good reason for being in that part of Hastings. It was a place where everyone knew everyone. His aunt was as black as his mother and, not for the first time, he wondered who his father might have been as his own skin was so much lighter although his hair was truly West Indian with close, tight curls.

She was dragging on a cigarette and the air was thick with the smoke. The flat was stained a yellow hue to her chain-smoking and there was an unpleasant stale tobacco smell that hung heavily everywhere.

'He looked alright though?' She had asked the question several times but seemed reassured with the same answer being given on each occasion.

Rab nodded again, he looked around the small sitting room and the mess the police had made. Their search had revealed a pile of unwashed clothes, but little else. They had not even tidied up, the officers were not convinced that they had left it in a worse state. The drawers in the small cupboard that acted as the shelf for the oversized plasma screen were haphazardly pulled out and the whole thing looked as though it might topple over at any moment.

His Mother sat next to her sister and their likeness was evident. His mother was dressed in scruffy tracksuit bottoms and had an overlarge hoody enveloping her body. It was clear that she had no clients soon. She, too, was dragging heavily on a cigarette. She looked tired and ready to argue. Rab felt that this was the same as usual, his whole life was always just seconds away from a shouting match.

Rab told the story of the morning again and left nothing out except how he got a lift home. He just hoped that his mother didn't notice her anti depression tablets missing anytime soon. All three of them suddenly jumped at the loud knock on the door. All the flats have recently had double-glazed doors fitted as part of a new form of health and safety regime and they looked incongruous in the scruffy setting of the flats that had been built in the 1960s. But the door seemed to shake with the resonance of the blow.

The knock soon became a very big thud and his auntie Cristy went over to the window, gently pulling back the tatty net curtains that hung loosely from a rail that needed fixing.

'It's the Blokes,' she whispered and pulled back, but too late.

'Hey, you bitch, let us in or the door is coming down.' The thudding became louder and far more menacing.

Rab half stood and his first reaction was to run but there was only one way in and out of the tiny flat. He was caught with indecision and looked towards his mum for help.

But all he saw was her face full of horror and she beckoned for him to hide behind the large settee that dominated the small room.

'Rab, just get behind that, it's best they don't see you again today.' The boy reacted quickly and slipped behind the settee with is back hard up against the wall. He felt his mother sit on it and push it hard up against him. Wincing with pain he managed to hold his tongue.

His aunt was already at the door and opened it with a flourish.

'What do you lot want? Isn't it enough that my Jason is in Eastbourne nick, what more do you want?'

The two large men pushed past her without comment and were in the sitting room within a second. Eric grinned when he saw Rab's mother.

'Ello darlin', not working? Fancy earning a quick tenner?' He made a rude gesture and Rab felt the old red anger course through his body, but he was trapped and was only able to contain his voice by thrusting his fist into his mouth.

The teenager was unsure what was happening as the room seemed strangely quiet. Unbeknownst to him his auntie had signed to the two men that there might be hearing devices planted in the room. She was making obvious gestures and had pointed at the light switch. This had stopped the two men in their tracks and both were miming to each other and then, in turn, making cutting motions to the two women. Both slowly backed out of the room and left the flat.

Cristy gave a huge guffaw and her sister actually fell off the settee clutching her stomach. Both were crying with laughter and fear in equal measure. They hugged each other and, still snivelling, gave a small smile, their eyes meeting.

Cristy came to first and said one word, 'Rab' and both rushed over to the settee and pulled it away from the wall. Their tears of just a minute ago soon became a wail as they saw the foam coming from his mouth and the wild look in his eyes.

In Rab's hand was a broken brown paper package. Its end slowly spilled the valuable cocaine.

The boy had spotted the package projecting out of the back of the settee and because his arms had been pinioned he had used his teeth to grab it and tug it out. But he had inadvertently swallowed some. He could see his mother and auntie shouting at him but just wasn't able to open his mouth. What he did do, though, was to start laughing, uncontrollably.

The ambulance arrived within twenty minutes. The paramedics were quite used to this particular journey and the dangers it usually presented. They had to lock the ambulance securely before starting their run up the four flights of stairs, they knew from bitter experience that the lift would be broken and their van rifled for anything if left unattended and open.

Rab had lost consciousness by the time of their arrival and the hysterics of the two women complicated any actions they tried to perform. But they knew that Rab had to get to hospital quickly.

When they got back to the ambulance there was clear evidence that someone had tried to break into the back door. Quietly swearing under his breath the driver helped his associate load Rab in.

'Mrs, er, Mum … do you want to come with him?'

But Rab's mother shook her head, her face was thoroughly wet with tears and whilst she knew that Rab was in danger, she also knew that she and her sister had work to do.

'You take my boy, I'll be over to the 'ospital soon'. Rab's mother gestured for them to leave.

Carrie, the other paramedic shook her head in disbelief and sat next to Rab. The insulin solution was already attached and she carefully placed the oxygen mask over his face. All her attention was on the teenage boy.

The ambulance let out its piercing wail and set off for the hospital. The two women hurried back to the flat, they would have very little time but they had lots to do. Both of their sons were in danger – there could be no evidence of the drugs in the flat. The sisters set to work.

Two hours later Ms Jerome was staring at Rab's face. He looked at her little baby once more and she cautiously moved her hand to take his as it lay outside the bed sheet. He was going to be alright, she'd been told.

'All right,' she wondered aloud, 'I wonder what that means.'

She felt the tap on her shoulder and slowly moved her head round, the appearance of not only the police but Social Services as well hadn't surprised her, but the fact that they had come to the hospital was appalling.

'Yeah, I know, I know, right darlin' you want to speak to me – lets go.'

She cast one look back at Rab and gave the briefest of smiles as she noted his heavy breathing. He was her little man no matter what happened. She followed the three women out of the ward and into a small conference room near the Sister's office.

'I'm police liaison officer Maureen Tuttle,' a short plump woman said and extended her hand out. Rab's mother looked down at it and gave a sigh.

'Darling, I ain't going to shake 'ands with you, not now not never.' She shook her head incredulously and then she looked at the other women.

Maureen looked abashed and quickly withdrew her tactile offer of friendship. Her tone hardened as she introduced the other two women.

'This is Naz Singh from East Sussex Children's Services and her manager Susan Strange.'

Liz Jerome looked at the other two women, she craved a cigarette and wanted to speak to her sister in equal measure. The last thing she needed was another lecture about how to bring up her son.

She did sit down as suggested and struggled to take on all that was being said to her. Later, when she recounted it to her sister all she could do was repeat small phrases and ideas.

She did remember her scream and that the nurse and doctor appeared out of nowhere and had injected her with something that took away the pain. But also took away her dreams.

4

DECEMBER 1485

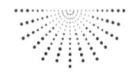

'The Tudor rose was invented to symbolise the unity that had supposedly been brought about when Henry VII married Edward IV's daughter Elizabeth of York in 1486 entwining the two warring branches, the houses of Lancaster and York together,'—**Dan Jones**

St Haura Village December 1485

Mary felt the laughter leak from her. The sun felt hot against her bare arms and she pushed them into the barrel of water once more. Bending her head, she deftly bit into one of the apples as it bobbed on the surface.

'That's not fair, you used your hands,' cried Mark. As her little brother stamped his feet in indignation both Richard and Rufus burst into laughter at his antics.

Mary picked her head up and still using her hands took a large chunk out of her red and green apple. She felt alive and so very happy.

Richard picked up the barrel, trying to show off his strength, and accidentally upended the contents all over him. It was

Mary's turn to squeal with laughter and Rufus struggled to contain himself. Mark pointed at the big boy and shouted out 'look at Richard, he's wet his breeches.'

Richard, his face hot with anger and embarrassed at being laughed at by the other children did what he always did and struck out at Rufus. His rival for the attentions of Mary.

Rufus, holding his face, now red with the blow shouted out 'my father will hear of his, you, you – ORPHAN!' Rufus, so normally calm and mild mannered was as angry as Richard. Both boys wanted to look good in front of Mary and a fight was only just averted by the arrival of Sir John.

'Now then children, stop all this, I will not tolerate it'. Matthew and Mary's father had been watching from afar and had high hopes of a good marriage between his daughter and Rufus, a distant cousin. But his support of the Plantagenets had generated high debts and he was worried about a dowry. Not for the first time he regretted taking in his old friend's son as his ward. He felt that Richard was a bully.

Tutting under his breath he shouted out 'bring me my birch.'

Richard looked up and his face, crimson with anger, now turned a shade of white.

One day, he thought, one day.

∽

Splat! A large piece of dung hit Mary full in her face and she quickly awoke. The dream of that Summer's day, long ago, quickly dispersed.

She jumped up and moved the two paces so that she could see out of her glassless window. The children scampered away with one turning and giving a quick jig, imitating someone who had lost their mind. The other children laughed and started to copy him. The face of the nun was barely visible to them as it appeared in the small space.

Mary wiped the mess from her face and felt a tear trickle down her face. She was cold and hungry and had only a vague awareness of what day it was. She hoped that Beth would be alone soon. She wore a wimple but her dress was dirty and the thick cotton lay heavy on her. It was now tatty and needing repair. Its fine stitching had started to unravel and it was merely a relic of the wealth and position she had once possessed.

Her only visitor was Beth, who rarely missed a day no matter the weather. She would hand through the small hatch a change of underclothes and anything else that she could provide. Mary's diet of rich meat from her previous life had now changed to coarse grey bread made from rye and barley. The beer she drank was strong and usually gave her a headache.

The new nun yearned to go outside her confinement, to stretch her legs and feel the weather upon her face. Her new home seemed to grow smaller each day and so she was struggling with the winter months. The small cell was already blackened by the smoke and Mary was forced to ration the twigs and wood.

'My Lady, My Lady are you awake?'

Mary smiled and replied, 'Beth, that's my favourite voice, come in front so that I may see you'.

Her servant bobbed up before her and Mary gave a gasp of shock and surprise. The old woman sported a massive black eye and she was leaning heavily on a self-made stick that she was using as a crutch.

'Beth, Beth, what has become of you? Oh Beth, who has done this?' Mary's rage overcame her cold and hunger and she clutched at the outside of the small window.

The bruised woman looked up at her mistress.

'My Lady, I will talk to you from within if I may,' and she quickly ducked out of sight.

Mary quickly crossed to the other side of her cell and pulled back the crude curtains that Beth had so carefully made for her. The small chapel was dark inside and she could not make anything out at first. Then she saw the stooped figure of her servant and heard the clunk/switch of her crutch and long dress.

Beth lit a taper and Mary could now see more clearly the damage the servant had endured. She felt her face moisten and she tried not to cry aloud.

Beth stood a little way away from the hatch and furtively looked up and down the small chapel.

'My Lady, Sir Richard's men have beaten me.' Beth had been determined to be brave and shrug off her injuries, but seeing her Mistress, she felt her resolve weakening.

'A curse upon them.' Mary could not contain herself and, realising what she'd said, quickly raised a grimy hand over her mouth. She was in a place of worship and meant to be a nun! She fell into a stunned silence, not trusting herself to speak anymore.

Beth looked worn out and downtrodden. Once a fierce and proud woman, she had undertaken her duties willingly and without complaint but having to visit her mistress every day and make her food, do her washing and even take her excrement away had started to take its toll. To add to her woes, gradually, over the past three months, many of the villagers had started to shun her. The local ale house had even developed a type of mead called 'The Mad Women.'

She was now friendless and the small amount of coin that Mary had given to her was rapidly running out. The servant was scared for her own life let alone for her mistress. But the previous night had been the worst. She had been dragged out of her small one-roomed hut at the edge of the village and paraded through it with many of the women who she had previously felt had been friends laughing and jeering. She was made to hold a sign up with a crude drawing showing that she too, was mad.

Beth dropped her crutches and cautiously made her way closer to Mary. She had to look up and could only see part of her mistress's face. Undoing the loose shawl from her shoulders she passed up the bundle. Within it were clean drawstring drawers which were quickly grabbed by Mary. The nun moved away and Beth could hear the younger woman changing out of her dress and putting the cleaner clothes on.

Beth gave a low groan of pain whilst she waited and sorted out the small cauldron of mixed vegetable soup. When she saw a small hand protrude she passed it up.

'Be careful Mistress, it was hard gained.'

Mary quickly drank down the dark concoction and gave a gasp of recognition as she looked beyond Beth and at the man who was now standing behind her. Beth turned sharply and stared at the image.

'Father, I thought not to see you here.'

Father Thomas made the sign of a cross and held aloft his taper. He passed it over a long candle he was carrying and lit up the small area.

'Sister Mary and Mistress Beth.' He paused and, as Beth had done, looked around him cautiously.

'I have news and I hope it will bring a change to all our fortunes'.

His face was illuminated by the candle and there was a hopeful look in his eyes. The nun and Beth looked at him expectantly. But before he could speak Beth lowered herself onto the rough floor, her body ached and the two mile journey had worn her out. No one had been into the small chapel since Mary had decided to incarcerate herself there and the few villagers that ever attended now sought their religious solace at the local village church. The small altar had gathered dust and there was a dank smell that had no incense to clear it away. The last service held there had been in August. The cold and dismal winter dusk was nearly upon them.

'Don't mind me Father, I'll just rest here.'

'How could you allow this to happen, you should feel ashamed.' Mary had found her tongue and was quick to chastise the priest.

Father Thomas did feel a terrible guilt about the neglect he had allowed Mary and Beth to endure. But the fear he felt about Sir Richard had overcome these concerns. However, the scroll he held in his hand had jolted him back to realising his obligations.

Mary peered out of her cell, the months of solitude had robbed her of her ability just to chat and interact with anyone. The young vivacious woman who had entered into this different way had changed, altered beyond recognition. She waited for the priest to talk.

Thomas explained that he had a letter from the Holy See. The priest could not contain his excitement as he stated that the Archbishop of Canterbury, Cardinal Bourchier was going to officiate over the marriage of Henry VII and Elizabeth Woodville.

Mary gave a gasp. Elizabeth had once been her childhood friend when she had spent some weeks at court with the girls playing in the long and empty halls of the Tower of London. The two girls had hit it off and had spent much time together. Mary had been in awe of Elizabeth's father, Edward. His towering height had made him even more magisterial to the little girl and she had been transfixed whenever in his presence.

Mary's father had not fallen into debt at that time and whilst his small landownings brought in little wealth it had been enough to ensure that Mary and her brother were raised in what passed for luxury at that time. His problems all began when his friend died penniless and Sir Thomas had taken his little boy Richard as his charge. Even making him the ward of the Griffin family. Sir John had even taken many of the debts too. But his own gambling addiction and desire to live beyond his means had taken a heavy toll in equal measure and by the time Edward IV had died in 1483 the wealth of the Griffins had dwindled to almost nothing.

Mary tried to shake the strong memories of her childhood away. She had been dwelling too long on yesteryear and she now tried to focus on the priest. He obviously had something important to say but his usual reticence in her presence had made him tongue tied. Suddenly, after a long and heavy pause, the words spurted out.

'Mary, Elizabeth will wed the new king, and soon', he could not help but give the briefest of smiles; he wiped his mouth and fervently wished that he had brought some water, he carried on, 'She wants to come and see you whilst travelling to the Tower. She and Henry have been visiting his family in Wales. So much has happened since the battle.'

Mary gave a start and confusion spread over her still pretty face.

'But, but why would she marry this man?'

Beth struggled to stand upright. She too, had been listening intently and was confident enough to enter into the conversation.

'Women do what is needed, My Lady, we always have.' Her sense of duty had always overcome everything else.

Father Thomas nodded vehemently.

'The houses of Plantagenet and Lancaster will now be as one.'

He tutted he saw that the taper was running low; struggling to control the long sleeves of his dour looking cassock he looked around the small chapel forlornly for some kind of substitute light. Mary could see his dilemma.

'I have no other light Father, we shall have to carry on talking in the dark.' As usual her pragmatism shone through.

As she said that the light gave a last pathetic flicker and all three of them plunged into an all-enveloping darkness. The late November winter gave scant warmth and Mary was tiring from standing at the small window.

'Father, how does this marriage affect my fortunes? Lady Elizabeth and I both have lost loved ones, but our friendship was a long time ago.'

'Your Lady, my apologies, I cannot read the scroll now, but I will tell you what the main part said.'

∼

The scroll was from the cardinal and had been sent to the local bishop, who had visited Thomas at this humble cottage that morning. The arrival of such an important man had caused quite a stir and many of the villagers were gossiping about what it might mean. The Lady Elizabeth had heard of Mary's decision to become a nun, but when she had realised that Mary had become an anchorite nun she had insisted on coming to the tiny chapel. Anchorite nuns were exceptionally rare and she had been both worried for her old friend as well as curious.

∼

Thomas had spent some time with the bishop, an old and fussy man who wanted to ensure that the new king was happy with him. Even the priest could see the political ramifications. The bishop had aspirations on acquiring more land and wanted to appease Henry in every request. For him to visit Thomas was both unusual and a clear message. Thomas knew that he had an important task.

The priest had gleaned from the bishop that Elizabeth was willing to marry Henry and felt no animosity towards him. All of her anger and hatred was still directed at the memory of Richard the Third. She felt that he was responsible for the deaths of her two brothers, who had mysteriously died in the

Tower of London in 1483. Richard had been her uncle and a man that she had never liked nor trusted.

Mary allowed the priest to wind through his conversation with the bishop without interruption. She had no real hopes from the visit except to allow her some respite from the bullying from the local village. She knew that she would die in this confined space. She felt as though her obituary was already written.

After Beth and the priest had gone Mary allowed herself a brief indulgence of a small candle. She shivered in the confines of the cold, bare cell and with fingers that shook with nerves as much as the effects of the winter. She took out the small figure of the griffin from its tiny hiding place. She had chiselled out a small crack in the plaster and had disguised the space as best she could.

She half stroked its familiar shape and, stooping low to retrieve the small whittling knife, she finished the scraping on the side of the wall. Her familiar actions allowed her a chance to think through the conversation.

Perhaps Elizabeth would bring some succour after all. She remembered her old childhood friend fussing over her two little brothers and the two girls used to giggle about how silly their siblings were. All three were now dead, all victims of the War of the Roses. She mused some more and concluded that this marriage might well work and bring much needed peace. But that would be too late for her.

Mary bent her knee and gave her usual prayers to God, it was the same each night. She blessed Beth and gave the most horrendous curses to Sir Richard. She desired, above all else, for him to be dammed for all eternity. It gave her life purpose if it meant that he would suffer.

It was only a week later that the future queen visited the chapel. She came with only a small guard and little fanfare. Some of the villagers had cleaned the small chapel but it still looked bedraggled. Father Thomas had helped them and the company and idle chatter amongst the women had helped Mary overcome her depression. She could hear the women talking to each other and she had shouted out questions to them about what had been happening in the village. They had been willing to engage with her. It hadn't taken long for all of them to have laughed at some long-forgotten memory jointly shared and all of them wistfully yearned for Sir John to be back amongst them. One young wife, easily pregnant and had some close to Mary's window and whispered a story of Sir Richard riding though the market and the horse reeling up at the sound of a bear being baited. Richard had been thrown off and had landed in a pile of dung. Mary found herself smiling over the next few days at the idea of it. She felt as though she had seen it herself, such was the vivid image she had created.

Mary was craning her head looking outside one day, hoping the woman would come back when she heard a familiar voice saying, 'So, this is where you've put yourself.'

Mary turned suddenly and rushed to the other window that looked into the chapel. Elizabeth was peering into her small cell and drew back as Mary ran across. Elizabeth held a long candle and her face caked with white makeup looked ghostly in the half light. She wore a wide dress embellished with red and green stones that shimmered in the shaded part of the chapel. Beside her hovered her lady-in-waiting who gasped in disbelief as Mary's face appeared in her small hole. There was a flash of recognition between the two women.

Elizabeth beckoned to her servant to leave them and stood to face her once childhood friend.

'Mary, it is true then, you are a nun,' She paused and raised an arm in a wide swoop, 'in these circumstances?'

Mary smiled and croaked out an affirmative. She leaned further out and tried to see down the church. She was thirsty and Beth had not yet come to deliver her freshwater or mead.

'My lady, do you come alone?'

'Yes, of course, I trust no one and feel friendless, although I have always counted on your friendship and ... loyalty?' She finished off her sentence with a strong emphasis on the question. She came closer and lowered her voice.

'Have you heard that I am to marry Henry, the upstart from Wales?'

Mary craned her neck even further so that her lips were as close to Elizabeth's face as possible.

'I have, is it a match well served?'

'Ha, the marriage is one that I have no choice in at all. It is being rushed and must appear something that I crave. Perhaps it will bring peace? I don't know, there are rumours already that there is a boy in Ireland who states he is my nephew!' Elizabeth was close to tears and murmured 'I miss my family, even my Uncle!'

Mary had a strong memory of her father, brother and Richard arguing over the gossip that Richard the Third had been responsible for the disappearance of the young princes.

'But he killed the boys, didn't he? Everyone has always said so'.

'Perhaps, dear Mary, perhaps,' Elizabeth drew back slightly and checked that the chapel was empty. She had a strange look on her face, as though she wanted to say more on the matter. Mary craned her head even further.

'I have little time here and word of everything I do gets back to Henry,' she gave a shudder and whispered, 'he has taken me, twice.'

Mary pulled her hand before her mouth and her eyes reached out to Elizabeth.

'He wants a child desperately, and forced himself upon me, but no one would believe me if I claimed it, he is a vile man. His breath smells and he has so few teeth.' Elizabeth's eyes looked pleadingly at the nun.

She leaned back and gave a brief laugh and Mary had a vivid recollection of them as two girls talking about who they would marry one day, both of them had wanted big strong men with good teeth.

'But you are to be married?' Questioned Mary, she was still struggling to absorb that Elizabeth been raped.

'My Dear Mary, I have to marry him now, I can hardly wait whilst my bump might grow.'

'But, I have brought you a present as well as wanting to see you.' Elizabeth held up the candle higher and it cast a different shadow over the two women. Mary looked up and saw the timbered roof, glancing down she saw that Elizabeth held a small cloth bag out, Mary had to pull her head back so that one thin arm could reach out for it.

'You will always be my friend and if I do have influence at Court I promise to try and help you if I can. But I wanted to give you this to keep within your…' she paused and struggled to describe what she felt was a living hell, '…your confinement?' She laughed and added 'perhaps we both have a confinement.'

Mary took the small bag and replied 'I am here now and here I will remain.' she pushed her head out again and tried to add resonance and resilience to her voice.

'This is my home and my church, I will know no other.'

Elizabeth leant forward and just managed to catch part of Mary's face with her lips.

'Be safe little friend.' She drew back and with a flourish pulled her dress round in a twirl.

'I will help you as best I can, pray for me and pray for the children I will bear.'

Elizabeth pulled the strong wooden door back and was gone.

Mary sat back on her small pile of straw and gently caressed her cheek, still feeling the soft touch of her old friend's lips. Then grimacing with pain she pulled at her Habit and felt the familiar drip of her menstrual cycle.

'Back again are we?' And she sought out some rags. Her cell was dark and she slunk down with the cramps and made her mind focus on her prayers. The small bag remained clutched in her hand but it did not dominate her thoughts. She thought instead of the dream she had once held dear, of marrying, bringing strong children into the world, of re-establishing her family name. She wondered if she would ever dream again.

Elizabeth was met by her lady-in-waiting as she emerged from the chapel. A priest was lurking nearby and further off was her carriage with two of her servants, Henry VII's men.

'Priest, why are you here, about to administer a service?' She looked around with a sardonic look, the small building had a few forlorn trees nearby, but otherwise showed no sign of care, nor parishioners.

'My Lady, the Lady Mary is shunned within the village, the local lord has great influence'. The priest looked steadfastly at his feet and was shocked at his own brazenness.

Elizabeth gave a great grunt and hurried away towards her carriage, leaving her lady- in-waiting scurrying after her. Once she had reached the small door she turned abruptly and shouted out, her voice firm and strong, 'Let it be known in the village and to all villeins, yeomen and peasants that if anyone befouls the nun that lives within those walls the archbishop himself will take reprisals and...' she paused for dramatic effect, 'I WILL NOT TOLERATE IT.'

She opened the door and within just a few moments the carriage set off. The driver whipped the horses and the two servants riding nearby. Their swords clearly visible and their faces grim.

The priest hurried down towards the village and passed three women who were practically running. He caught them up.

'Father, Father, did you hear the queen?' Squealed one and Father Thomas stopped.

'Those three must have been hiding nearby,' he mused. He realised that Elizabeth must have seen them and her shouting had been for them to hear and pass on.

He gave a brief smile and carried on his way towards his own small, humble cottage sited next to the larger village church.

IF YOU FAIL TO DREAM. ALL YOU HAVE LEFT ARE NIGHT...

∾

The next day the Priest returned up to the chapel and was unsurprised to see a number of their villagers had gone up there too. Some were tidying the grounds and the door was open.

Its tiny interior was lit by a number of candles and the alter at the end was being righted, having been turned on its side for months.

He moved towards the small curtain and gently tugged them apart.

'My Lady, My Lady are you within?' He stood back and waited. After a few moments he heard a rustling and breathed a sigh of relief when he saw her face appear in their space. He knew that the two women within the chapel had stopped their tidying and were keen to see the nun.

'Father, Father, What's all this commotion?' Her voice sounded querulous and the strong outspoken woman who had entered this confinement just a few months ago seemed to have gone forever.

And then he heard her fall, there was a loud crack as her head struck the stone wall.

5
SUNDAY 24/11/2018

'He who opens a school door closes a prison.' - **Victor Hugo**

Rab woke up with a throbbing headache and a distorted memory of the past twenty-four hours. He rubbed his head gingerly and stared around his new room. The built-in bed was hard and uncomfortable and all the furniture appeared fixed to the wall. The skirting boards seemed high on the wall and the door looked heavy and unfriendly. There was a tatty poster hanging down from the one plain wall, its Blu-Tack bulky behind the picture of a pink unicorn.

Staggering upright he found more memories started to flood back to him but, more importantly, he had a hunger pain that pushed out all other concerns. His stomach was almost painful. He tried shouting but his voice was croaky and lacked any real depth.

Someone must have been listening outside the door as there was a knock followed by the unmistakable face of Ms Arnold appearing as ever with a warm smile dominating her face. She stepped back into the corridor and spoke to someone else that Rab could not see. She seemed to be reassuring the other person and then she came into his room properly.

'Hello Rab, gosh you've been asleep for over five hours, I bet you are ravenous.' She paused at the door of his bed and looked concerned. But her infectious grin soon dominated her face once more.

'What the ... Rab stopped himself just in time as he slowly righted himself. He stretched and felt the pull of the blue jumper, he looked down and saw all his clothes, he was fully dressed. Slowly all the memories started to come back. They were blurry and he sat down whilst he concentrated. There was the journey in the ambulance, the social worker holding his hand, the strange smells. He recalled hearing slow but clear words. He shook his head as though to jog them all together and remembered the acronyms, so many of them, he looked up at Ms Arnold and she asked, 'Want to talk about it all?'

Rab, normally a usual taciturn teenager, nodded and started to tell her what he could recall. She helped him make sense of it all by gentle interjections and giving strong nods of appreciation when he strung some of the thoughts together.

Rab now understood that there had been an application for an EPO, an emergency protection order, as it had been explained to him, and how the court had granted it, but just for forty-eight hours. It had 'ordered' that he be taken to a secure children's home at Hilldowne based in Harlingen. Rab had heard of such a place and he thought he'd once met a girl who had gone to it a few years ago.

He recalled how the ambulance had passed through the gates surrounded by a high fence with occasional lights fitted into it. The ambulance had pulled into an enclosed courtyard with the gates being pulled close behind it. Rab remembered feeling groggy and nauseous, still feeling the effects of the cocaine he had taken he supposed. He tried to explain to the young teaching assistant that he thought himself removed from all around him and had watched himself as though in slow motion and through a purple haze. Ms Arnold sat on the edge of the bed and gently took Rab's hand. The motion was entirely caring and he welcomed the warm touch. Sucking in more air he continued to narrate what had occurred.

He had been met by a large old man who had resembled any image of Father Christmas that Rab had ever seen. His friendly face and red cheeks had appealed to Rab like no other man had ever done. 'Father Christmas' had explained that a thorough strip-search was part of the regulations and Rab had allowed the intrusive process to be completed with a surprising benign calm. His new uniform had been fresh and clean and he had been shown to his room. After a whilst Ms Arnold put a finger to her lips, smiling, she said 'let's talk more, but it might be better to go and sit in the common room.'

Rab had a questioning look in his eyes as they left his room but followed her meekly.

He sat down with Ms Arnold, or Jenny, as she was called in Highdowne and she explained that she worked part time at the children's home, doing some weekend shifts.

'After all, my job as a teaching assistant isn't paid THAT well!'

They were relaxing in a small but meticulously neat communal area. Rab had not realised but the home's education provision, the Hilldowne school, was run by St Thomas's school as well. Mr Carlyle might well pop in to see him on Monday morning. He carried on listening intently and learnt that the home was made up of three wings and had provision for seven children. Each had their own bedroom and all the furniture and even the fabric of the building was robust, in case anyone 'kicked off'. The far wing was the school, with a tiny sports hall and five classrooms, one of which was a small hairdresser's station.

'Shall we have a tour then?' Asked Jenny and she held up a bunch of keys and what she explained to Rab was 'a fob – which is like a key.'

So Rab wandered round with Jenny as she showed him each room. He was impressed and stared at each new part in disbelief. The new building had only been open for five weeks and there were some building materials yet to be tidied away from the central courtyard.

'So, what is an EPO again?' Rab asked Ms Arnold as they sipped some squash from plastic cups.

'It's an Emergency Protection Order.' Jenny Arnold gave another beautiful smile and carried on making the drinks for the other two teenagers in the tiny common room in one of the wings.

'A Family Justice of the Peace can grant it for a limited time.' She reached up and grabbed a biscuit tin.

Rab nodded rapidly, showing his need to keep on eating. He now knew that the JPs that he'd seen deal with Jason were similar to a family one, but different too.

'So, how many of these places are there then? I mean, they must cost a bomb!'

'Well, I think there are only a few.' Ms Arnold wasn't too sure and didn't want to make a number up. She turned back to the issue of Rab's temporary order. She watched him grab yet more biscuits.

She laughed and added 'your EPO is for seventy-two hours and then you'll probably go home, or...' She paused and carefully said 'somewhere else.'

Rab crunched his way through the ginger nut. His usual rage against the world appeared to have deserted him and he was just curious.

'Won't I go home then?'

'Well, you might, but it depends on how safe it will be for you.'

She walked past a tiny pale girl who was anxiously sitting on a nearby stool listening earnestly to the conversation.

'How long have you got here Maria?'

Maria gave a shy smile revealing a quick glimpse of small broken teeth, which she quickly hid behind a raised hand. Her voice held a strong northern accent and its squeaky resonance made it almost impossible for Rab to understand her. She explained that she had another week and then hoped to go back to Newcastle. She looked so frail and vulnerable that Rab felt immediately protective towards her.

The only other child in residence sat in sullen silence staring at the massive plasma TV screen. Rab genuinely couldn't tell if it was a boy or a girl. There was a lot of long hair that had been washed but still looked disheveled. Rab noticed that both hands had bright nail varnish, but what face could be seen appeared as though it needed a shave.

Normally Rab would have challenged the teenager and quickly established a pecking order, but he already knew that he would be number one. In this small kingdom he was 'The King'.

He had been fed, was warm, clean and felt physically safe. More importantly, he was with Jenny Arnold. Right where and right now, life was good for Rab Jerome.

∼

After just two hours the full impact of his situation became real to Rab. He was a prisoner, only be allowed to go where he could see. To leave the area where the children slept involved him having to have a member of staff with him at all times. The new building now had sophisticated locking systems which could only be operated by a Fob He asked to go to the tiny gym to shoot some basketballs and had to wait thirty minutes for there to be someone free to go with him. Ms Arnold had finished her shift and gone home. She had promised him that she would be back tomorrow and her replacement care worker appeared brusque and exhibited the classic signs of just not wanting to be there.

Rab waited whilst Big Tim, the new care worker swiped the fob and the two of them went into a small airlock; eventually emerging into the corridor that led to the school.

'So, what's the school like, know what I mean? Asked Rab as they walked past two classrooms. Each had a PC in the corner and a large TV screen mounted on one wall. Big Tim laughed and gave a shrug. He had been asked to be called Big Tim as he obviously worked out, with his muscles showing through his tight-fitting jumper. He led Rab in the gymnasium, which was only slightly bigger than a badminton court. There was one basketball ring mounted against a wall. Tim went to an adjoining stock room, soon emerging with two 14 kg dumbbells. He kicked a basketball out which slowly rolled over to the boy.

Rab started to take a few shots and soon realised that the net was much lower than usual, he was making every single one. Within minutes he was bored.

'Hey Tim, can we go back now?'

Tim looked up from his bench. He scowled and shook his head, returning back to his exercises. He was soon lost in his grunting and concentration.

'Tim, hey big man – I am done – see'. Rab started to walk over to the figure of the care worker, now lying on the bench, all his efforts into repeatedly raising the dumbbells up and and forward.

Tim stopped again and looked up at the teenager who was now standing over him.

'Rab, that is your name isn't it, Rab?' He stood up, his muscles seemed to bulge after the workout and he opened his arms expansively.

'Rab, you asked to come here, so here you are,' he paused for dramatic effect. It was as though each word had been said with strong deliberation and Rab felt as though he was being talked down to, as usual.

'You are safe here, but I'm not your servant, you'll go back when I'm good and ready and not before.'

Rab thought about his chances, he'd blown up a lot at school but always knew that any restraint would merely hold him and he'd likely not get hurt, too much. He was in a strange place and there was nowhere to run. He started to feel the blood pumping around his body and his breaths started to become shorter. His instinct was 'fight or flight' and, as there was no option of 'flight' he could feel the adrenalin coursing through him. All that had happened over the past few hours, his overdose and now this, being a prisoner, meant that he was a kettle and the boiling point was due at any second.

Tim had placed the dumbbells back and turned to Rab, without really looking at him, he gestured that Rab should follow him and made to leave the gym. The explosive leap from Rab took him by surprise and temporarily knocked the big man over. Rab had pushed Tim, not realising that he would fall over. Instinctively Rab ran, he passed the classrooms and approached the glass door. Too late he remembered that he had to have that fob. Banging on the door he felt the long-awaited tears course down his cheeks. He was trapped and just didn't know what to do.

'Rab, Rab, it's OK.' Tim was behind him, talking softly.

Rab tensed, waiting for the expected restraint, he only turned when nothing happened. He faced Tim, frozen in unhappiness and uncertainty. Tim pointed behind him and he turned once more, through the frosted glass he caught sight of another man coming towards him, not Father Christmas, but merely a portly chap with a white beard.

With his heart rate starting to slow down Rab watched as the door opened and the unit manager stood to one side to allow Rab to pass.

'Hello young man, I heard that you had awoken, you've got a real fan with Jenny Arnold, she speaks very highly of you'. The older man posed no threat at all and oozed a tranquil calm.

He then looked beyond the teenager and asked. 'Everything alright then Tim?'

The large care worker nodded and, whilst the incident was probably recorded on CCTV, Tim was too embarrassed that the teenager had actually pushed him over to ever mention that it had ever happened.

'Rab, please come into my office, I've the best hot chocolate making machine in the world there.'

∼

Rab was soon seated in a well-furnished office, everything was new and neat except for a battered desk and a swivel chair that had wheels which caught on the carpet.

'Rab, I don't think you know my name, it's Mr Martin, I'm the manager here, I look after the care staff and the building generally.'

Rab accepted the proffered hot chocolate gratefully and looked around him.

'Ah, you can see the brilliant artwork I have here,' Martin gave a theatrical flourish around the wall and Rab could see three tatty looking drawings/paintings that a child had obviously done.

Mr Martin continued 'That picture of a rocket was done by Maria, who do I think you've met?'

Rab gave a mirthless smile and had retreated into being quiet and on edge. He recalled that this was 'The Father Christmas' that had stuck his finger up Rab's bottom yesterday, as part of the self-styled 'search'. Rab was starting to remember, and not all the memories were pleasant ones. He turned slightly on his chair and the wheels stuck again, giving it a theatrical shove, he looked down, the carpet was plain and rough looking, but very new.

'Why is it that you got new stuff everywhere but have this old chair?' Rab tried to spin round and gripped the arms tightly to help him.

Mr Martin appeared very relaxed and sipped his own chocolate.

'When the Home Office gave East Sussex the funds to build this I tried to put all the money into the wing, where you slept.' Mr Martin didn't appear perturbed at the teenager trying to spin in the swivel chair. He stayed behind the desk and merely kept talking. His tone was moderate and calm.

'So, I had to keep some of the old furniture, you are a bright chap and have noticed that there are only three wings?'

Rab looked back at the old man, his interest piqued now. He had known that Ms Arnold had only told him so much.

'Yeah, why is that? Seems weird.'

Mr Martin sat back, he was able to look at Rab now, who appeared calm and focussed. The manager had been watching Rab and Tim through the monitor earlier on and had foreseen the incident; he knew he had arrived just in time and had made a mental note to see Tim about his conduct later. For now, he continued.

'The Home can only cater for seven children, if this is successful, then the missing wing will be added. You see Rab, this children's home isn't for anyone that's committed a crime, it's to keep them safe. There are other homes around the county that have both welfare and YJB Beds'

Rab was fully attentive now, his large eyes were fixed on the Manager

'What's this PJB then?' He asked.

'YJB'. Mr Martin leant back a little, he had known that Rab would be fascinated and now had an opportunity to find out more about the teenager in front of him.

'Youth Justice Board,' he smiled expansively.

'It's when a youth over the age of ten has committed a crime and has to be sent to a children's home that's secure, it's a bit like a prison and it is usually for a fixed term. There's only seventeen in the country and only five of them are just for welfare beds. This is a welfare one'.

He paused as he could see Rab calculating and knew that a question would follow.

'What's welfare then? Why am I here?'

'Welfare is when someone has not actually committed a crime but just needs some protection for a while, ' Mr Martin continued to talk about some of the young people that stayed. Rab was astonished to hear that they had come from all over the country. By piecing together what he had been told Rab soon realised that Maria had probably had some horrible things done to her and that's why she had been put here.

'Right young man', said Mr Martin, 'shall I take you back to the common room?'

Rab nodded, his mind was full of all that he'd learnt and, whilst he still felt trapped, he had regained some of his trust in the staff here. He followed the old man through the freshly painted corridor, into the airlock and arrived at the residential wing. Maria looked really pleased to see him and shouted a big 'hello' from behind her hand.

She was sitting at the large table and had been engrossed in more artwork. The other resident had gone back to their bedroom.

'What are you doing there darlin'?' Rab wandered over to the small, thin girl. He thought that she must only be eleven or so. He now knew that some important politician, 'what was it,' he tried to remember.

'The home secretary' he said aloud and felt himself blush.

'What's that?' She asked.

Rab laughed and finished his thinking 'the Home Secretary is the only one that could take Maria from her home and put her here because she is under thirteen'. The Manager really had said a lot.

'Nothing', he lied to her. He then carried on. 'Now, I know what this is.' And Rab peered closer to her drawing, she was just adding some colour.

'Wow, that is some griffin,' he said and gave a low whistle. 'Why are you painting it blue?'

Maria was as pleased as punch. She had been frightened at the home and whilst she had been there for a few days, she hadn't been able to talk to the other resident. She liked this big teenager. She liked his confidence and how he smiled. Most of all she loved his curly and bushy hair.

'Griffins can be any colour and I like blue.' She sounded sure of herself.

Rab was in his element and he settled next to her and they talked about how a griffin should look. The girl explained to him that it could be called a gryphon but it would still have the body, tail and back legs of a lion and the head and wings of an eagle.

Rab felt himself relaxing and he told Maria, someone that he'd never met before, about the building at the end of his school drive and how it appeared full of drawings of griffins. her eyes grew wide and she wanted to know more. Rab started to draw what he had seen.

∼

The next morning, after breakfast, Rab was taken to Mr Martin's office once more. He was surprised to see Mr Carlyle sitting in the ancient swivel chair. Mr Martin asked the care worker to leave them and stood up to move towards Rab.

Mr Carlyle stood up too. Rab felt his defences rise and rocked back on his feet, he had slept well and had been really impressed with the shower, all that hot water! But now, were they going to grab him?

Both men saw Rab's reaction and stepped away. Mr Carlyle spoke first.

'Rab, it's OK, we were just going to greet you.' He held his hands up and open and Rab relaxed. Both men sat down and Mr Martin gestured that the boy should sit too.

'Well Rab, I'm guessing you are surprised to see me here?' Mr Carlyle began and then sat back surprised as Rab started to speak. The teenager poured out all that he knew, about the Home, the residents and even the connection to the griffin. The headteacher was so used to Rab being taciturn and surly most of the time this young man before him was like a revelation.

IF YOU FAIL TO DREAM. ALL YOU HAVE LEFT ARE NIGHT...

Both men sat back and listened, they had been talking about Rab before he had come in and it was clear that they felt he had some good in him. The headteacher had never seen him so garrulous and he could not help but smile to himself.

Eventually the three of them got round to discussing what would happen next. Rab was quite pleased to hear that he would stay at Hilldowne for another three days and then he might be returned to his mother. Social Services would meet with him here and report back with their recommendations. Rab sat quietly through this, he wasn't too sure that he wanted to go back to Hastings, but then again, he didn't know what he wanted.

Mr Martin explained how his mother and aunt had refused to explain how the cocaine had been in the sofa and that the police were happy to add it to the charges already levelled against his cousin Jason. The two men made no reference to the Blokes and Rab wisely held his counsel.

Mr Carlyle finished off by asking if Rab was ready to go to school?

Rab laughed, there would only be three students in that tiny school but he quite liked the idea of being with Maria for longer. He felt like her big brother.

~

The school started at 9.00am and the three students were escorted down the corridor and up to its entrance. There was even a sign up over the door 'Hilldowne School'. A very smiley lady met them and led them in. Even though Rab had been on a tour and even played in the gym, this felt different. The three of them sat on a comfortable bench in the main foyer and he realised that there was another large TV screen mounted on the wall opposite to him. The smiley lady introduced herself as Mrs Ham, two other adults sat amongst the three children. They were the teaching assistants. Rab looked around and recognised Big Tim standing over by the other corridor, they gave each other a raised eyebrows look of acknowledgement.

For the next fifteen minutes Rab had an assembly, just like he would have had at his usual school. Led by Mrs Ham who used the interactive TV with real skill. Rab hadn't seen one like it and soon realised it was a notch above the half broken interactive whiteboards he had been used to.

The morning passed with traditional lessons, English, maths and even a brilliant food technology one. Rab really enjoyed himself as he was willing to engage with the staff and got a lot of attention. The third student, after a while, did start to acknowledge Rab.

'What are you bro?' He asked under his breath as they moved from one classroom to another.

'Is you a girl or a boy? I don't mind either way, I jus' want to speak to you without disrespecting you, innit.'

Marvin gave a wry smile at that and whispered back.

'I don't know myself yet, but I hope to soon.'

After they had made their 'healthy option' pizzas Rab noticed the scars on Marvin's arms. He had seen lots of them before, on other people, and gave a small grimace. Even when things were at their toughest he hadn't resorted to hurting himself. Marvin noticed him looking and quickly pulled down his sleeves.

Rab shrugged and turned to Maria. She was concentrating on cutting her pizza to represent a griffin. Rab laughed and thus drew Marvin's attention.

'What's that?' Marvin asked.

'It's a griffin,' Maria and Rab said in unison and Ed, the teacher came over.

'Wow, it really looks like one, impressive work young lady.'

Ed pulled up his own sleeve and revealed an intricate tattoo of a small griffin. All three students were mesmerised. The talons looked so lifelike and it curled up Ed's arm. Rab had a brief vision of the one he had seen on Eric, thankfully the two depictions looked different.

'Did you know that there was a family who owned most of the land hereabouts called Griffin. They even had a family motto showing it.'

'Yeah, I think I know where that might be too' said Rab and he talked about his school. There seemed to be some connections that were making some sense? He thought about that as the lesson continued.

At lunchtime they left the school and went the seventy metres back to their residential wing. It seemed mad to Rab, but that is what they did, they went to school and then went home for lunch.

Once back at the common room Mr Martin was waiting for him.

'Rab, when you've finished your sandwiches, hmmm- is that home-made Pizza Maria?' He paused and gently took a slice from her proffered plate.

He turned back to Rab. 'You've got a visitor, a little unexpected, so, only come to my office when you are ready.'

He gave a small nod to Anne, one of the care workers. It was obvious that she would have to accompany Rab when he was finished with his food.

Rab crunched through his peanut butter sandwich and wondered who was waiting to see him. He had an unpleasant thought that it might be the police.

6
MONDAY 23/2/1501

'Sing a song of sixpence, a pocketful of rye;Four and twenty blackbirds baked in a pie.When the pie was opened, the birds began to sing,
Wasn't that a dainty dish to set before the king?
The king was in the counting-house, counting out his money;
The queen was in the parlour, eating bread and honey;
The maid was in the garden, hanging out the clothes,
When down came a blackbird and pecked off her nose.'

- Unknown. Probably early 16th Century

February 1501

Mary could hear the children chanting and struggled to come to her senses. They seemed to be playing directly outside her window, she concentrated on the words and felt the growth of a smile spread across her lips.

She struggled upright and felt the urge to urinate. She sat on the uncomfortable wooden bucket and let out a massive fart.

'She's awake I tell you,' said one girl

'Yes and she's just farted,' shouted a boy.

She heard them giggling and she could not help but join in. It had been a long time since she had laughed and the effort to stop just made her fart more!

'Sister Mary, sister Mary, it's Arthur and Anne here.' The children shouted out in unison.

Mary finished adjusting her dress and reached across for the basket with her soiled clothes. She found the stick that had now been provided for her and carefully pushed the basket through the window.

'Here you are my lovelies.' She waited until she felt the weight go from the end of the stick and then felt the familiar and very welcome metal bowl being hoisted onto the end.

'God bless you and your mother,' she cried out and clutched at the bowl of pottage eagerly dipping some bread into the mix. She sucked noisily at the crust and, not for the first time, worried about how loose her teeth seemed to feel.

The nun had not aged well and the attractive young woman who had decided to not only take Holy Orders but to incarcerate herself within her own church had become stick thin and had a yellow pallor to her skin. The blow to her head from her fall all those years ago had left a vivid red mark across her forehead and she was prone to the most violent of headaches still.

'Sister Mary, are you finished yet, as we have to return to the village.' The twins, whilst happy to go and bring the old woman what she needed, were reluctant to stay up near the chapel for too long.

Mary went to the window and peered out, they were the grandchildren of Father Thomas and the boy looked particularly like the old priest. Mary had been quite shocked when she had learnt of his indiscretions and still could not believe that the plump and attractive Ruth had fallen for Thomas. But she had forgiven him more than once over the years. She knew that she owed him her life, her sanity and was one of the few links she had with the outside world.

'Now what's that rhyme you've been chanting?' Mary loved the children to stay as long as possible and was keen to keep them talking to her.

The twins stood a little back now that Mary had appeared. The smell that emanated from the small cell could be overpowering, not just from the excreta that was occasionally merely tossed out of the window, but from Mary herself.

The boy, Samuel, piped up. He was the braver of the two, and, having been born a full hour before his sister, felt that he had to take control. He knew he had to shout as the sister had grown a little deaf over the years. Mary was thirty-three now, but looked nearer to fifty- three.

'It's about the queen and the king.' He paused and looked up at the face peering out at him. The chapel needed some repair and the wall that protected the nun was starting to tilt a little as it butted against the chapel. The few gravestones that had been there under Sir John's time and before him hadn't been added to and many had sunk to being barely visible. There was ivy that trailed up the walls and the pathway that led around the side and to the old oak door which was badly in need of repair.

'Did you Know her, Sister Mary? My grandad says that she visited here. A long time ago.'

Mary shook her head and tried to clear her mind. She got so confused these days and couldn't grasp what the boy was saying. Her head had been hurting more recently and she wondered if she had heard him correctly.

'Queen Elizabeth and King Edward, why would they be counting money and having their noses pecked off?' She sounded a little cross and was suddenly worried that the children might head off back to Haura Village.

Mark's sister gave another giggle and looked at her brother in amusement. They were familiar with the old nun's ramblings and had been told by their grandfather to be kind.

'The blow to her head all those years ago had scrambled her brains,' he had kept telling them, 'but once she had been an important person, a lady of distinction.'

Well, it was true that sometimes she could be lucid and other times she was vague and unaware of where and who she was. The two eight-year-olds fidgeted with frustration and Mark carried on.

'Sister Mary, remember now, Queen Elizabeth is married to our Lord King Henry the Seventh.' He recited the fact with a look of concentration on his face and his sister nodded her head earnestly.

The old nun shook her head and, as if by magic her memories seemed to click together in quick succession until they became clearer. She frowned with distaste as she suddenly caught a smell of herself.

She looked further than the two children and could see dark clouds gathering on the horizon. There was a strong wind too. For a brief moment she was back being Lady Mary of the House of Griffin. The Lady of the manor and daughter of

IF YOU FAIL TO DREAM. ALL YOU HAVE LEFT ARE NIGHT...

Sir John. With a voice that would brook no argument she shouted out, 'you two, get home before the rain comes and thank your mother for the clothes and food.' She gave a smile that had once been beautiful.

The nun settled back and tidied away the basket. her small space had more decorations now. There were some blankets hanging from the walls which had helped with the insulation and made it a lot warmer. She had a crude and small table too, replacing the old one that she had been forced to burn one particularly cold winter. And the rushes she used for her bedding had a covering of goose feathers tied up in a bag. Her pottery urn had some water in it and she had a few nails banged into the stone walls. Her spare wimple hung from the one nearest the curtained window. It now looked as though someone lived there, albeit in exceptionally cramped conditions.

She paused and pulled out her long hair, her one remaining vanity. Her decision not to cut it as was the custom when becoming a nun had been made merely due to the lack of scissors such had been the haste for her to escape Richard all those years ago. Taking her crude wooden comb she dragged it through her hair, it was still dark brown and not the lustrous red of the queen. She mused again on her visit as she began the lengthy process of braiding it. Her hair had become very long over the years and no one ever saw it. Nor did Mary ever see her own face. There was no looking-glass mirror.

She knew that her visitor was due soon, it was such a rarity that she had the event marked down firmly in her mind. she had been lending some thought as to what she would say. Fingering the ring on her right hand had always helped with her thinking, it was too loose below the bottom joint and she was able to wriggle it about. But her arthritis was advancing too quickly and she was no longer able to slip it off. However, she knew the tiny inscription by heart and had little need to see it. She sat down and let her mind drift back to that brief hot summer and her time at court, way before the battle of Bosworth. Elizabeth's brothers are dead now, slain in the tower by her uncle. Her own brother and sweetheart died too. She shook her head a little and returned to the present. She stood up and stretched, her back making an ominous cracking sound.

Then she allowed a smile to trickle over her furrowed lips. The sad memories were replaced with one that always made her smile. Richard, the self-styled Lord of the manor and owner of the Griffin heraldic symbol, was dead too. His end from the pox had been very unpleasant and protracted. She had tried to hear every grisly detail from anyone that had visited her. Mary had praised the prostitutes who had dealt him such a blow again and again in her prayers. This happy thought always brought a look of contentment and she moved to look out of the window.

Outside, the small chapel was now appearing more like a normal building than a self- styled church. The shape of the cross which all churches had to have was hard to distinguish now partly due to part of the eastern transept having fallen down after some strong winds from years before. It badly needed some repair. The small face looking out of the glassless window was hard to make out from any distance.

The Manor House too was lacking care and attention. Richard had died without issue and the King, true to his reputation, had not replaced the lord, instead keeping the revenues from the itinerant tenants for himself. No one lived there now and few had recourse to visit it or the old nun that lived within one of its buildings on the estate.

∽

After her contemplation Mary had fallen asleep. She awoke after a few hours and, again, had to shake her head until it cleared. The nun wondered if she had experienced another fit, they seemed to come without warning and always left her feeling drained. The fits had added to the belief held in the village that she was mad, Mary preferred to think that it was God's way of talking to her.

'Sister Mary, are you awake now?' The young man had crept close to the window and his cheerful countenance and obvious wealth looked at odds with the setting. The bright red stockings were very fashionable and he held a wicker basket in one hand full of apples and pears, in the other was a leather satchel.

Mary heard his voice and popped her head out scanning him intently.

'Are you young Thomas?' She licked her lips, 'Son of Sir John More, the lawyer?'

He gave a brief bow and a cheerful smile.

What a pleasant young man, she thought to herself. She gave him an approving smile and beckoned him closer.

'Sister, may I come forward, my business is not for all ears.' He spoke quietly and confidently and Mary nodded her assent.

'Young sir, it may be better for us to speak once you are inside, or are you nervous about speaking truthfully once inside God's house?'

Thomas More blushed and stammered a reply that showed he had been quickly and easily unnerved. His face showed no guile at all.

'I will speak to you once inside and I promise that my words will hold the truth.'

The young man made his way round and opened the large wooden door with difficulty. The old metal hinges groaned with the struggle. Thomas entered cautiously and was surprised to see what his nose had led him to believe. There were bales of hay stored inside and even a wooden plough that needed some repair. He struggled to find any indication that this was a church at all.

He ventured further in and gave a start when he saw Mary's face watching him from behind a small crack in the short curtains that were half way up one wall.

'Shall I give you a tour?' She gave a mischievous grin and beckoned with her head.

'See, we have an altar, but there are no services held here now, the front was removed four years ago. And there—' she thrust her head forward and behind him.

He turned and saw the faded artwork of the Old Testament story of Samson and Delilah.

'—I helped paint that when I was a child, I wanted to be just like Delilah and have my own Samson.' She paused and looked directly at the young lawyer. 'But he died on Bosworth field with my brother, but I expect you know that?'

Thomas turned and saw the nun's piercing eyes twinkle, he knew that what he'd been told was accurate. She had a keen intellect but an odd sense of humour. He could not conceive what her life must be like and his natural curiosity to ask questions was held back by his desire to complete his task without rebuke. It was rare for his services to be required by the queen and the secrecy she had insisted upon had made him realise that it's importance was obviously high.

'Sister, I was unsure what to bring out as a gift and thus followed the advice of my mother.' Thomas held up the basket and started to take it toward the nun. Mary took the basket quickly and was soon biting into one green apple but grimaced as one of her teeth gave her a swift reminder not to. She gently nibbled instead.

'I cannot stand here too long, young man, so be quick about your business.' Mary allowed the sweet juice to run down her face and gleefully licked her lips. She noticed Thomas staring at her intently.

'Well Master More, what is it that fascinates you so, ask and I'll tell you no lies.'

Thomas held his tongue and, instead, rummaged through the satchel and produced three sets of papers, some quills and a small pot of ink.

'Ah, your tools of your trade, good let's get to work.'

Thomas bowed his head once more and began to explain his purpose in coming to see her. Mary was transfixed. The young man was handsome and engaging. It had been too long a time for her to remember what it was like to have the attention of such a man. But she held her mind to the task and only asked questions as and when she was unsure what he meant.

Thomas explained that the queen was suffering from a series of maladies and was worried that she might not live much longer. She wanted all her affairs to be in order of preparedness. Thomas had been instructed to tell the nun about Elizabeth's children in particular. Mary was astonished that Elizabeth had borne eight children.

'Eight you say?' 'Eight is so many!'

Thomas had produced a sweet-smelling cake from a parcel in his bag and the nun eyed it appreciatively.

'What's that? What have you there?'

Thomas delved again and held up a knife as though one of the mummers might have done it if it were a show. He bowed and smiled.

'This is a Simnel cake, made by one of the king's own cooks. The man has created a masterpiece and I believe one that future generations will enjoy at this time of year for generations.'

He cut a hunk off and passed it over to the nun who gratefully sat down with it. She found standing for too long tiring as the window was just a little too high for her to see through without going on her toes. She bit into it and the sweet marzipan tingled on her tongue making her give a brief sigh of contentment and enjoyment. She now had a chance to assimilate all the information and felt a strong sense of jealousy at her old friend.

'Eight children,' she said again.

She shouted out 'But only four remain alive, is that not so Master More?'

Thomas too had sat down on the messy floor near the hay. He had found talking to just a head more than disconcerting and he worried about the echoing words he felt his speech had generated in this odd setting.

'So – Arthur is to marry the Spanish infanta, Mary is betrothed to the King of France and Margaret to the King of Scotland.' Mary repeated her newfound knowledge. Such details were not known by the villagers and Mary felt privileged. She was sad about the other children who had died in infancy and was wistful about her own lack of children. That dream, for her, had died a death many years ago.

She stood up once more and asked shrewdly 'This cake, its name is Simnel you say?'

Thomas looked up and jumped to his feet, he had set a small trap to test her understanding and was pleased to note that she had taken the bait.

'Yes, Sister, Lambert Simnel no less.'

Mary nodded and smiled. She understood what must have happened but carried on anyway.

'I presume that the young pretender Simnel was kept on in the kitchen, say, as a turnspit, to act as a deterrent to any other pretenders to the throne?' She looked quizzically at the lawyer, who was starting to grin broadly.

'And this young Irishman actually became such a good cook that he made this, this thing of deliciousness?' She too was starting to grin.

'Sister, you have it all, that is it in its entirety.'

'So, what happened to Perkin Warbeck, did he become a farrier?'

Thomas stopped his smile with an instant frown.

'No, Sister, he was hung, two years ago.'

'Ah!' Said Mary, understanding even more.

'Ah, so the king is becoming more assertive and less willing to counter any possible challenges with a light touch?'

Thomas nodded and took a bite out of his own cake. He had been unsure what to expect and had only brought it at the direct behest of the queen. He was pleasantly surprised.

'Well, do you have a pie full of blackbirds now? What else lurks in that bag of yours?'

'I have something which I think will match something you have?' Thomas said this last question quietly and kept his gaze steady.

But the nun was still deciding whether she would trust this young lawyer, she needed to know more about him before she would reveal her secrets. She tried to keep the conversation light for a few minutes longer.

'So, is the queen in the larder eating bread and honey?' She had an image of Elizabeth as a striking woman with wide hips but no real extra weight. Her best feature had always been her red/bronze hair.

'And you've no mention of the other son, Henry, is it?'

Thomas raised himself with a little hesitancy and realised that he was being tested. The wily nun would only talk more openly if he were to do so first.

'The queen has a little more presence than she used to, Sister. I fear the supply of honey does, occasionally, run a little low.' He tried to show a more relaxed face and was relieved to see that the nun found his answer amusing and reassuring. He still felt uncomfortable in the dusty and odd building and wondered whether the news he was to communicate would change her life forever.

Mary made up her mind at that moment and knew that she had to trust the lawyer more than might be wise for her.

'Wait there, eat some more cake, but no peeking.' Her voice was that of the lady of the manor once more. The nun turned back and deftly crouched down towards the bottom of the external window. The crack that she had created all those years ago had not been as she wished and the work of the Master Mason Simon had rectified the problem for her. It had been his skill three years ago that had created a simple but easily disguised cache hole. The brick that she was able to loosen with a simple turn of a pivot that had to be placed into a crevice made the removal of a larger piece of masonry easy. Within just a few moments she had retrieved the leather pouch and within it the bag that the queen had given her over sixteen years ago.

Simon had completed the work willingly and had sworn to keep his task a secret and whilst he had created the secret compartment from outside no one would have been able to see his craftsmanship. The only payment he had been willing to accept was to be remembered in her prayers. Not for the first time she thanked God for putting Simon's work near to Haura village. he had been naturally curious to see how the young woman was that he, himself, had bricked up. His brief trip up to see her had generated the task he had so readily completed for her.

Mary reappeared back at the window and showed the bag to the lawyer, quickly pulling it back as he looked like he was hoping to snatch it.

'Thomas, I have few things of importance within this cell and you will not have them without a fair exchange. You have been sent here in secret. I know that you have no major position at court and thus the queen must have chosen you due to the faith she has in you, but, also, because you can move about without causing interest to prying eyes.'

The nun was aware that she was gambling on his honesty and was relieved when she saw the truth of her words on the young man's face. He bowed graciously.

'Sister, I must make haste and am aware that my fine horse tethered outside may be causing interest. You have it right and the queen said that you would understand too.'

He paused and delved once more into his bag, producing the last of his treasures, a bag similar to the one the nun had.

'I have news that will upset you My Lady,' he unfurled one of the documents and read aloud. The Latin made little sense to Mary and whilst she was a nun, she had never learnt to read and speak the dead language. However, her knowledge of the scriptures was superb.

'Sirrah, I know not what you say, you'll have to just tell me what the import of it all is.'

Thomas stopped and apologised. He was a keen follower of the new humanist movement and was determined to have more written in the vernacular language of all Christian countries so that all could understand God's word; but many legal documents were still written in Latin. But he was, also, a devout Catholic and powerfully aware that the contents would cause distress. He drew himself up and told the nun that the consecration of the chapel allowing it to be a church had not been completed properly. The queen had managed to obtain the documents that stated this and had kept them safe over the past ten years or so. But she knew that she was ill and expected that she might die sooner rather than later.

'She is ill? How ill?' Mary interjected. She was absorbing this information and it came as no great shock to her. Everything had been so rushed back then and Father Thomas had never been blessed with any great intellect. She believed she was within a church and trusted her devotions to God were well founded.

'No, she has no direct malady, but she does suffer from sweats and bowel pains.' Thomas had been expecting a question like this and he repeated what he had been told.

'She is bled regularly but knows that the damage from childbirth would have left her beyond repair.'

Mary nodded and questioned the lawyer more. Thomas explained that with Richard's death and the reversion of the Griffin land as well as Richard's own to the king made her own position helpless.

'I am Sister Mary and this is my church, am I not an anchorite nun?' She summed up all her questions into a simple statement and was pleased to see Thomas nod as he passed up the document.

'Sister, if this document is destroyed, then, yes you are, my conscience would be clear.'

She grabbed the old vellum parchment and, without glancing at it, threw it behind her.

'Master Thomas, this is news but not news that I take any great notice of, but I thank you and the queen for your assistance.' The nun then held up her right hand and showed the ring.

'I was never married to our Lord in a ceremony but the queen gave me this herself and the inscription tells me that I am, indeed, in God's House.' She rotated her hand and forlornly tried to remove the ring, unsuccessfully.

She then pulled her own document out, a much smaller one and the seal had broken over the years. The veracity of it could have easily been doubted in a court of law. Thomas reached out for it and saw just how thin Mary's arm was as she allowed it to be taken from her. She had kept that safe for so many years and was surprised just how upset she was to see it go. The presence of it had made her feel important and needed, somehow.

Thomas glanced at it and realised that it had been written in the queen's own hand. it briefly said that she had been raped and was being forced to marry against her will. If that document had ever come to light it would have brought many more pretenders to the throne and possibly have toppled the Tudor dynasty before it had taken hold.

'Tell me Thomas, how soon was Arthur born after the queen's marriage? Mary asked a question to which she knew the answer.

'Eight months, Sister, eight months.' The Lawyer spoke solemnly and hastily poked the document into his bag. It would be burnt in the queen's presence.

'Arthur is a poorly young man and it is unlikely that he will survive much beyond marriage.' Thomas spoke almost absentmindedly as he adjusted the satchel and picked out the item from his bag.

'If he dies, what will happen to the infanta? That would mean only one son left to inherit?' The nun mused as she concentrated on the bag that the lawyer held.

Thomas retrieved the small gold talon and after showing it solemnly to the nun, carefully placed it back in the bag and passed it up to her. She gave a gasp of surprise and delight and retrieved it to study it closely. It resembled her own relic and she held both in one hand. She felt a tear trickle down her face and a sense of release go through her body. It was the half that Richard had torn from her father's neck.

'My Lady, that is a key question, and the Bible has different views about it, but I suspect that she will remain in England.'

But the nun wasn't listening and felt exhausted by the encounter. She seemed drained and wilted a little as she leant upon the edge of the hole.

'Master Thomas, I think that we have concluded all that we needed to do. Please do visit me again and I will look forward to eating such delicious cakes once more.'

Thomas doffed his cap and finding his most charming smile once more said that he would come again and would bring a present of a book he hoped to write one day. A book explaining what a society should be like, a wondrous place. But the nun had slipped down and he was left speaking to an empty place. She clutched at the two presents he had brought and held them close to her breast.

7
WEDNESDAY MORNING 23/11/2018

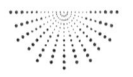

'They say a person needs just three things to be truly happy in this world: someone to love, something to do and something to hope for.'
— Tom Bodett

By the third day Rab was desperate to leave the close confines of the Secure Unit. The food was brilliant, the staff quite caring but the lack of privacy was overwhelming. He had cut himself shaving and there had been a massive backlash of forms to fill and people to see. Just the sort of bureaucracy he hated.

'I never meant to cut myself innit!' Rab was confused by the attention. He was used to utter indifference from his mother. But here, everything was scrutinised.

'It's just that we have to be so careful,' explained the manager. His likeness to Father Christmas had now totally faded and he appeared like just another old and tired man. Only with a shaggy white beard and a red nose due to too much alcohol.

'I know, I know, but I'll never top myself, not never, know what I mean?' Rab rapped his chest in what he hoped was a meaningful and masculine way.

'Shall I get Big Tim to show you how to shave?' asked Mr Martin.

Rab nodded forlornly, he had thought that he could do it, but the gash on his cheek had been a wake-up call for him and his sense of independence.

He was going to be released that afternoon. A taxi was booked for 2.30 and he was being allowed to go to a temporary foster placement. The police had interviewed him twice but his memory of the incident at his cousin's flat was vague at best and he had no intention of explaining why he had been behind the sofa or what he had seen. His story was that he had just bitten into what he thought was some food and then had had some kind of fit. The detective had been very sceptical and had looked meaningfully at Rab as he had left.

'We will need to discuss this again, but if you do decide to remember anything, here is my card.'

~

His mother hadn't come to visit either but she had tried to FaceTime him. He hadn't been allowed his phone and the link had been due to occur in Mr Martin's office. But the boy had refused to speak to his mother, he wasn't sure what to say, so he had made Mr Martin talk to her instead. Rab was embarrassed at the number of swear words but not surprised at her repeated questioning of the manager about what Rab had been saying. In the end the Head of Hilldowne had been forced to end the conversation in an abrupt manner.

'Don't worry, she is always like, like … like that'. Rab was trying to make the older man feel better, but he could not put into words what his mother was truly like. She might have been genuinely finding out how Rab was, but then again, she might just have been concerned about what Rab might have said.

'She's always, annoying like.' Rab concluded and gave the manager a massive winning smile.

Mr Martin looked up and could not help but smile back. He wondered what would happen to Rab in the future. He had seen that Rab had hidden qualities and had been impressed with the quick and easy influence he had managed to exert over Marvin and Maria. All the care workers and education staff had taken to the outspoken young man too. Far too often, though, the manager lost touch with how the children faired once they had been returned outside and away from the safety of his unit. On too many occasions he had wept when reading the papers he was sent about the children that came to stay and, more recently, the whisky bottle in his top drawer had required being replaced more than before.

Rab swaggered out of the room. He had tried not to think too much about his cousin, the drugs or his family and had, rather, focussed on the immediate: having fun lessons at the school and really nice food, with lots of it! He gave an involuntary grin and rubbed his tummy. Carole had been waiting for him outside the office. She gave him a cautionary wave as if to stop.

'Always nice to see you smiling Rab', she paused and went on. 'Much better than that usual grimace.' Rab gave an involuntary shrug of his shoulders and welcomed her soft touch to his arm as they negotiated a door.

What had made him laugh, though, was the social worker. She had been really nervous and had spent half an hour of the interview constantly looking over her shoulder as though expecting something dreadful to happen.

Rab had enjoyed that interview and had certainly played to his audience.

'Yeah, I only head-butted the bloke, his nose broke real easy.' Rab was in full flow, the look of horror on her face was just amazing.

'The claret pumped out, just like a…' he paused and thought about what he had learnt in English. Then, it occurred to him '…like a fountain,' he said triumphantly.

'Fella.' Big Tim was smirking too, but felt that he had to intervene.

'Stop telling the lady lies.' She could not see his face but she heard something in his voice that gave her a brief reality check. She tried to give a smile back, but her lips hardly twitched.

The three of them were in a small and immaculately clean conference room. She had arrived early and been unnerved by the strict security procedures. her handbag had been left in a locker and all she had was her laptop and a folder. Smoothing down her long dress she fitfully pulled at her short and uncared-for hair. She peered over her glasses at a bluff-coloured folder. Anxiety dominated every part of her.

'Relax Miss, I quite like it here, I even get on with the big fella.' Rab gave a nod towards the care worker, which was the same as a congratulatory pat on the back. Rab had warmed to him and the two of them had done some gym sessions together. The teenager gave the social worker his most sincere look.

Mrs Blake shuffled her papers and tried to complete her form. The questions were very standard and she already had some information about Rab on record, the problem was he often gave an answer that conflicted with what she was expecting. She didn't like being in the confined space with someone who carried the label SEMH and she took the acronym to accurately reflect how the person would behave. To her, anyone having Social, Emotional and Mental Health issues meant that they were unstable at best and dangerous at worst.

She had been busy doing a routine report when her manger had told her to go to Hilldowne as a matter of urgency. She struggled with alterations to a planned day and hadn't read all the information as thoroughly as she would have liked. She was ill-prepared and totally out of her comfort zone.

'So, you attend a special school, is that right?' She kept her eyes on her laptop and could not see the look of disgust on Rab's face.

'I ain't no loony, it's just my school innit, them teachers at my last school couldn't cope with me, but I ain't no div nor spas – GOT IT!'

Rab's temper temporarily got the better of him. He had seen the Variety buses collecting special needs children around his estate and he felt an urgent need to distance himself from that type of 'special needs.'

So, instead, he gave himself a smile of self-congratulation. 'I told that headteacher to go suck 'imself. That's why I was excluded. He just couldn't handle me.'

It was important to Rab that this was seen as a badge of honour and not something to be embarrassed about.

Tim looked across in a concerned way, the interview had to end, and, quite soon. All the danger signs were popping up and it was only a question of time before Rab said or did something even more inappropriate.

Fortunately, Mrs Blake seemed to type rapidly and then gave an audible sigh.

'Well, that's all I need Rab – thanks.'

She closed the lid firmly and started to tidy the loose documents. She seemed to have something else on her mind and had not really noticed Rab's belligerence.

'Is that all then Miss? Is it OK to leave this place now?'

Rab sounded plaintive and she was suddenly reminded that he was just a child. She looked up and gave a relieved smile.

'Yes, that's all OK now.'

She stood up and turned to go and having reached the door, she suddenly turned and gave a brief tilt of her head.

'Did you know that St Thomas's School used to be a convalescence home for wounded soldiers in World War One?' She pushed the protruding hand bell and seemed so much more relaxed now she was going to leave the small room and thus, the Secure Unit.

'Eh?' Said Rab. He looked confused.

'My school? Why was that?' Her random explanation had caught him unawares.

But before he could phrase any more questions the door was opened and Mrs Blake made a very swift exit. The boy stood up and stretched himself out. He clicked his fingers and gave Tim a huge warm smile.

'Any chance of another session in the gym?'

'No, Rab, we need to get you back for lunch and then ready for the taxi. Let's see if the others are back for their break.'

Rab only had a few minutes to wait before Marvin and Maria came into the common room. Marvin gave the briefest of half smiles and Maria waved her hand excitedly.

Rab had missed the last hour of lessons and had wanted to see Ed again. The three children sat together and the two care workers scheduled to be with them produced sandwiches as though by magic. Carole, the lead worker, bustled around and soon everyone was munching through an array of choices.

Maria ate the slowest as she still hated anyone to see her teeth. When her mouth was open she always ensured that her other hand hovered in front of it.

'Maria, ain't you seeing the dentist soon?' Rab, as usual, spoke as he thought and one of his many labels was Tourette's syndrome. But, on this occasion Maria took no umbrage at his brazen outburst.

'Tomorrow, ain't it Miss?' Maria's accent was also becoming easier to understand.

Carole nodded and looked up and towards the other carer. The three children smirked at each other, it was obvious to them that she fancied Sue, the younger Carer. They knew that the two of them would seek each other out for a quiet chat, predictably, it was within two minutes and Carole had half wandered over to where Sue was rummaging in a cupboard. Rab seized the opportunity.

'Well, did Ed say anything more?'

Maria nodded and her eyes shone with anticipation about Rab's reaction. Marvin now felt part of the team and he was fully attentive too.

Ed, their favourite teacher, had explained that the building at the end of Rab's school drive had once been a home for the Griffin family, about a zillion years ago, as Maria understood the date to be. Rab took a massive bite out of his sandwich and started to speak, his idea of good table etiquette was to eat as quickly as possible so as to get 'seconds'. His principle was always 'eat as much as you can, when you can.'

The other two children leaned forward and received a splattering of food for their troubles. But it didn't seem to bother them. They wanted to hear what Rab had to say.

'OK, I knew there was something special about that place. Honest, the little room I was in with Miss Arnold had loads of griffins sort of drawn around. It was weird, cos the roof was being repaired and I reckon the builders must have taken off a layer or summat.' He had forgotten temporarily about the titbit of information the social worker had mentioned.

Rab paused and took a slug of the orange squash. He leant even further forward.

'Did you two want to see it?'. If Mrs Blake had been there she would have ticked off another label, ADHD. Rab had always been impulsive and rarely had concerns about repercussions. He liked to think of an idea and then act on it straight away.

Maria nodded with an excitement she had not felt before in her lifetime. She was just eleven years old and had been the main carer for her mother: a woman who had found the basic things in life beyond her understanding. When Maria had been found, with the three men in a nearby flat, the investigations of the Social Services had shown that her mother was borderline imbecile on a grading chart. It is a category that no longer officially exists but one that professionals often used between each other to explain the inexplicable.

The decision to put Maria in a Secure Unit had been an easy one for the Home Secretary and the child psychiatrists knew that there would be extensive therapy needed before they were able to even scratch at the level of unpleasantness she had endured in her short life. Rab was the first person she had genuinely liked for himself and with whom she felt safe.

'How can we do that? We are locked up here, ain't no way out.' She looked imploringly at Rab and was surprised when Marvin spoke up. He had been so quiet before Rab's arrival and now she saw him for the first time.

'Yo' going to the Dentist tomorro', just go to the loo and disappear.' He still allowed his long and greasy hair to obscure his face but his one visible eye looked lively and there was a gleam in it. The three conspirators became locked into a small fantasy world and one that was dramatically better than the one they usually lived in.

'There you are then, easy innit,' said Rab and they whispered some ideas together. Marvin didn't want to run away and whilst he would miss the other two once they had gone, he wanted to pursue the appointments he had been told about that might help him decide just who or what he wanted to be. But he felt part of something and put forward more ideas. They whispered for a few more minutes, enjoying their precious freedom from prying eyes.

'Right, that's it, know what I mean.' Rab rubbed his hands in gleeful anticipation and was shocked when Carole was suddenly standing over them.

'What have you lot been cooking up?' She had a whimsical smile across her face and a slight tinge of a blush.

"And some good news Miss?' Rab countered her question with one of his own and he added a cheeky wink.

'Right young man, let's gather your things, your taxi is due very soon.' Her question about what they had been planning was dismissed from her mind. She gave a brief glance over her shoulder and sent a warm smile towards Sue. They were going for a drink after their shift and all her thoughts were on that rather than what the children had been so engrossed in.

～

Rab stared out of the back of the taxi for some time. The tall gates had opened and allowed the car to pass through and Rab tried to gain a glimpse of his new friends as he left Hilldowne but all the windows were designed not to face out onto the external courtyard and all he saw was the building.

The car manoeuvred its way out of Hillingdon and Rab noticed that it soon moved onto the road heading onto the A83. He appeared to be on his usual route to school.

'Hey bruv are yous taking me to St Thomas's?' The driver, a taciturn man with a sniffy nose glanced up into his mirror and shook his head.

Rab was used to drivers not talking and he smoothed his now clean clothes down. His tracksuit was a fairly new one and the Unit had dry cleaned it. The boy felt good and suddenly had an urge to look at himself in the mirror. He was surprised when the car turned off the main road and headed into the village of Mull but away from where he knew the school was. It negotiated a series of potholes and arrived outside a small and detached cottage. Waiting for him were two middle-aged people. Both had false smiles fixed on their faces.

As soon as Rab was out of the taxi the old man had exclaimed 'How do Rab, it is Rab isn't it?'

He had a jollity about him that was entirely for show and Rab took an immediate dislike to him. Rab had seen him before. He shook his head concentrated – it would come to him, he rarely forgot a face.

With a squeal of acceleration the taxi turned and left, leaving Rab standing with his small plastic bag holding his toothbrush and comb, all the possessions he had in the world right then.

'Come in darling, come in.' The woman stood back and led the way down a carefully maintained path and opened an ornate front door that was surrounded by ivy. Rab followed her in and felt the presence of the man behind him. The cottage was full of small delicate porcelain figures and each chair had some kind of stuffed toy on it, or so it appeared to Rab. He stared around him with a growing sense of unease.

There was a small staircase that led to the first floor and the man had to stoop so as not to hit his head. He kept up a monotonous range of small talk that required no answer or real acknowledgement. The floor was uneven upstairs and Rab felt as though he was on a boat, he had never been to such a place and it was like a horror movie to him. He was

IF YOU FAIL TO DREAM. ALL YOU HAVE LEFT ARE NIGHT...

starting to sweat and his safety barriers had started to drop. He felt more enclosed here than at the Unit.

The woman opened a bedroom door with a flourish and beckoned him in, there was a small bed with a floral duvet on it, a little washbasin was in one corner and a patterned wardrobe stood to one side. The curtains matched the bedspread and Rab could make out a strong smell of air freshener.

The woman, Mrs Stone as she had introduced herself, was evidently pleased with the room and her face fell when she saw Rab's scowl. Her husband was still in the corridor and, unbeknownst to Rab, was glaring at the back of Rab's head with a look of loathing on his face.

The Stones had tried for a child for over twenty years and the decision to turn their idyllic family home into a bed and breakfast had met with a similar lack of success. By the time they had reached their early fifties the decision to try short term fostering had been reached and was their only option. Rab was their first placement and John Stone, always protective of his wife, was very worried about taking such an obviously violent body into his home. But his business of 'event managing' had been struggling too, his life was not following the plan he had made for himself as a young man.

Robert Stone moved down the small corridor and faced the photograph of the smiling couple on their wedding day, a younger version of himself beamed up at the photographer. He clenched his fists once more and tried to slow his breathing down. When the LAC (looked after Children) agency had rung him last night he had been so relieved to have some income. The promise of fifteen hundred pounds a week had taken his breath away and he had agreed without properly consulting his wife. Now he had concerns, about her safety, how he would react and even whether Rab was worthy of his home. He glanced back towards the open door and could see his wife's face dropping with her own concerns.

Rab still hadn't said a word and, after a minute of awkward silence, all three trooped downstairs. Robert Stone was trying to put everyone at ease, but unsuccessfully, he picked up one of the stuffed toys and tossed it to one side with more violence than he realised. Rab and his wife watched the pink elephant dash to the floor and tumble over.

'Please do sit, Rab,' he gave what he hoped was an ingratiating smile, 'they all have a name you know,' and he gestured his arm in a wide swoop. His wife picked up the elephant and clutched it to her chest.

Rab's mind was a whirl and he had more questions than he could count. But his default position when being pushed into doing something he didn't like was to say nothing. He remained standing, a sullen look on his face.

Mrs Stone had sat down in her usual chair, not knowing what to do, she now stood, leaving all three of them standing in the small immaculately presented front room.

'Now look Rab, we've all got to get along here, so I may as well go through the ground rules from the outset, OK?'

John Stone had been a large, well-built man once but all he did now was the occasional round of golf. Too much comfort eating and pints of beer at his local pub had meant that his body had gone to seed. He felt Rab looking over him and saw the calculating look in the boy's eyes. He could smell the testosterone coming off the teenager.

Fortunately the dangerous atmosphere was cut through by the arrival of the social worker bustling through the front door.

'Don't mind me barging in, I saw that the door was open.' Mrs Blake appeared in a flurry of chaos.

'Ah good Rab, you've arrived. I'm sorry that I wasn't here to greet you.' She came into the room without realising what she was really entering.

' Ah, you've met Robert and Alicia Stone. That's good.'

She glanced round at the stuffed animals and china figures without really taking them in.

'What a lovely cottage isn't it?'

Her busy hair had, seemingly, sprouted more over the few hours since Rab had seen her. If it were possible, she appeared more haphazard than before.

Rab couldn't help but give a small smile. She absolutely oozed craziness but he knew that she was utterly lacking any premeditated danger to him. Rab started to relax and allowed his eyes to glance around the room more. Seeing a large Paddington Bear taking up an armchair, he deftly scooped the bear up and sat down.

'Hello Miss, how are you now?' The charm that Rab possessed had been turned on and the situation now seemed saved. Robert Stone looked relieved and half mopped his brow, his wife immediately started to fuss. The extreme tension of just a minute ago had disappeared.

'Mrs Blake, would you like some tea? Rab, I've got a Coca Cola for you, and' she turned towards her husband with an imploring look on her face, 'darling would you like tea too?'

She yearned to be active and, having seen Rab, now had to have some time to herself to assimilate the facts and have an opportunity to react to her own feelings. Rab was a scary figure to her and she had never imagined such a boy would be in her house. Her desire to have a child had dominated her life, and the miscarriage after miscarriage had robbed her of her looks and mental health. All too late she and her husband had realised that they were too old to adopt.

But she knew, having seen Rab, that she just didn't want this boy in her safe place, her home, a place she had created and put so much care into. Any pity that she might have had for him before his arrival had gone once she had seen him.

She filled the kettle and her hand was shaking as she popped the teabags into the pot. Try as she might, she could not stop the tears from flowing.

Inside the sitting room Mrs Blake was in her element, she wasn't looking at anyone and was oblivious of the atmosphere that prevailed.

'Now, I have the forms for you both to complete, yes, here they are.'

Rab got up whilst Mr Stone was busy looking at the paperwork and quietly moved out of the room. He passed by the kitchen and could see Mrs Stone sobbing as she stood by the sink.

I bet she never thought she'd have a black man turn up, he thought to himself. He was used to being rejected, this was just such another occasion.

Without making any noise he went through the pockets of the jacket hanging up by the back door. His luck was in and his hand soon felt the familiar touch of a wallet.

'Sweet man,' he said under his breath and softly opened the door. He'd had enough of social workers, of care workers, of his mum. It was about time that he sorted his life out his way. He strolled off round the side of the cottage and started off down the drive. Glancing to his left he had his second piece of luck. The old bike was leaning against a tree.

Meanwhile Mrs Stone made herself put on a sunny smile and took the can of Coca Cola through to the front room.

'Here you are Rab,' she called out, but all that met her gaze were her husband and Mrs Blake looking up from the scattered papers across the dining table.

'Where is he then?' She asked.

They slowly looked at each other and then watched in silence through the window as they saw Rab cycling off down the driveway.

8
MONDAY 19 APRIL 1918

'Everything depends on whether we have for opponents those French tricksters or those daring rascals, the English. I prefer the English. Frequently their daring can only be described as stupidity. In their eyes it may be pluck and daring.'

—Manfred Von Richthofen.

The triplane arced up and banked to Bob's left. It's bright red hue in direct contrast to the perfect blue of the sky.

'Right you Boring Baron, I've got you in my sights,' shouted Bob but the noise of his small engine coupled with the gushing air made his effort futile. His scarf flew back in one long trail and he pushed the hard button in front of him. The spittle of bullets from his machine gun spewed towards the bright red plane before him.

The pilot tried to hold his line, maintain his speed and cope with the huge vibrations that the wind flow created. He knew that his aim was poor and struggled to keep his plane from buffeting around too much. The famous triplane was

IF YOU FAIL TO DREAM. ALL YOU HAVE LEFT ARE NIGHT...

speeding away from him, arcing up and gaining enough height to make further efforts from the young pilot redundant.

Bob cursed under his breath and lost a crucial moment of concentration. A sudden wave of bullets coursed through his fragile Sopwith Camel and he noticed with alarm the plume of smoke that was billowing out from his engine. Trying to remain calm he adjusted his speed; the small biplane had been pushing its acceleration towards its maximum of 100 MPH, quickly adjusting his seating he now drew down on the throttle. He focussed on the job at hand.

It was bad and he knew it. He had known that the Red Baron always flew with some of his Jagdeschader or flying circus as he called them and cursed his own stupidity for chasing the Baron. They must have been just out of eyesight. Uttering a curse he glanced round to try and see if any of his squadron were near, but, then again, he thought, it didn't matter anymore.

Bob looked over and down, he had been flying directly over part of the Western Front and, with the height he was losing, every detail of No Man's Land was becoming clearer. The options were poor, the best being to try to land and make a jump for it at the last minute with the very least being two broken legs. His altimeter showed that he was losing height fast and he had to decide now!

He loosened his straps, parachutes were only vaguely talked about and the wing commander had told all the pilots that only a coward would use one. Everyone had to make sure their plane was saved. But Bob knew that this one wasn't going to survive. He wasn't sure if he would. Bob gave a grimace, he knew he was doomed. The air was rushing past him now. His stomach contracted with fear. He had never felt anything like this in all his twenty-one years.

The smell of the burning engine was overpowering, the heat from the fire starting to scare him with its intensity. He had to jump, there was, now, no choice... He tried to pull himself out of the tight-fitting cockpit and found himself bound up. It was hard to see as his warm leather jacket restricted his movement even further. But the problem was his scarf, it had become entwined around the seat and twisted across his mask.

Panic gripped him in its vice-like grip and he fought against it. The sound and sight of his plane crashing into one of the larger craters created a major distraction for both sets of troops as they watched from their respective trenches. The Germans and the British hated all aircraft in equal measure as the sight of them normally preceded a major round of bombing or an assault they called 'over the top', as the main use of aircraft was for reconnaissance.

Both sides even cheered and waved their rifles in the air as the plane landed with a thud and promptly burst into flames. The sky was lit up in a cascade of colours and this helped obscure the three heroic Red Cross orderlies clamber across the heavy and dangerous mud reaching the pilot who had landed in a pool of dirty water.

~

Bob regained consciousness three hours later, but the pain was too much and anything he tried to say was incoherent. He longed for the sanctity of sleep, but the pain rarely allowed him that crumb of comfort. The crude field hospital had rarely dealt with anyone from the Royal Flying Corps but they did recognise how severe the burns were and Bob was placed in a cot near the back and away from the other wounded. No one expected him to survive the night.

But he did, miraculously, and against all known odds. His clothes had to be cut from him the next day and his horrendous wounds were treated by one nurse. She adopted him and worked almost exclusively with the young pilot. Soothing the burns with a balm that she partly created herself and talking to reassure to him at every opportunity. The rest of the staff still felt that he was a lost cause and left the two of them alone.

Bob was bandaged up entirely and his face was totally obscured. It was as though he was anonymous, almost as though there wasn't a person underneath the swathes of cloth. His rank helped, that and his fiancée's contacts. The decision to send him back to Blighty was one made via a dignitary at Whitehall and the chief medical officer at the field hospital readily agreed. Surely the journey back would be the end of him?

Bob was unaware of the train, the stretcher onto the boat and then the ambulance from Dover to a small village north of Harringer in East Sussex. The overriding and burning sensation was the gripping and relentless pain. When he did try to think back over the long and involved journey, it was the gentle voice of the nurse and her constant soft touch that had been crucial. The single positive, almost dreamlike quality amongst the reality of the nightmare in which he lived.

∼

Could Bob truly hear her voice? He struggled to peer through the darkness to find her. His eyes were exposed now but he had experienced being able to focus his sight. His darling Edith, the second daughter of Reginald Castling, was she really here? or was it just another dream? Another one of life's jokes?

Bob fought through the pain that was always there, he sought to picture her, to recall the gentle graze of her lips as he stood by the train, his pilot's uniform scratching her as he bent to whisper in her ear. The look of pride on her face and just a faint touch of anxiety. The memories blurred as he managed to make a distinction between his memory and what was truly happening. Blinking as best he could he saw her father standing just behind her, a scowl on his face. They were in his room, it was happening.

'Bob, Bob, can you hear me? Bob, I'm so sorry but no, not this, anything but this, it's not fair on me, no, I cannot.'

Edith stood away from the bed, her arrival to the Manor House, a newly converted hospital had been within the past half an hour. She had been told that the injuries were horrific but had pleaded with her father to ensure that Bob could come back to Blighty, back home. She had then insisted on coming to the hospital as soon as she had been notified that Bob was back. But what she saw was beyond her wildest nightmares. Nothing could have prepared her for the catastrophe that lay before her. She fiddled with the simple engagement ring on her left hand. Her darling and dashing fiancé, his fine moustache and piercing blue eyes had gone. The charred and bandaged body on the bed was a stranger to her. She could not bring herself to go closer. Turning her head aside in disgust she held a dainty hand to her throat, the nausea swelled in her stomach and she felt herself retch.

Her father's disgust was only too apparent as he fidgeted by her side. His face a dangerous shade of puce as he struggled to contain his emotions, the overriding one being of anger. He had spent a small fortune and called in several favours to get the pilot to this hospital. In an act of decisive action he took his daughter's arm and guided her out of the single-bedded room.

The two nurses that had been hovering nearby left with them. Only one cast a look back at the pilot as he lay in his bed. His body immobile and what could be seen of his face revealing confusion and hurt. The four of them moved into a barren hall. Its wooden staircase dominated the building and all of them walked down the stairs. Edith was sobbing and an odd guttural noise was emanating from her throat. Her father held one arm almost brusquely whilst the taller of the nurses held the other arm gently, with an almost deferential touch. They all trailed into a large office.

A short dapper man stood up from behind a large desk festooned with papers. His pipe hung from his mouth and he hastily yanked at it, throwing it carelessly onto a glass bowl. He seemed to leap round the desk in his haste to proffer his hand towards Edith's father.

'Mr Castling, thank you for coming, I'm so sorry that I was not available to greet you and personally take you and…' he paused for a brief second whilst he looked at Edith. Her obvious distress seemed to alarm him too. He looked sideways at one of the nurses. She tried to answer but was interrupted by Reginald.

'Mr Fish, or is it Dr Fish?' Reginald Castling looked meaningfully at the shorter man.

'Yes, well, Dr Fish really.' He gave a short and nervous barked laugh. 'Please sit down.'

He gestured towards the two comfortable leather chairs that the two nurses were hastily moving across the room.

'Dr Fish, when I contacted you to bring my daughter's fiancée back to this hospital I expected you to act in genuine good will.' He paused to gather his thoughts. His face was red with anger and indignation. 'I even paid for this young girl to come with him at your behest.' He waved an arm towards the younger and shorter of the two nurses, who blushed at the reference.

'But that.' He took a deep breath and added, 'that creature,' he struggled to think how to finish his thoughts, then, with a burst said, 'should be shot, what you've got in there should be put out of their misery.' He gave a dismissive wave of his hand and, at the word 'shot' his daughter gave out a wail and rushed out of the room, hotly pursued by one of the nurses, the younger one who had recently come from France.

Dr Fish looked perplexed and held a soft, effeminate hand up to his mouth.

'Mr Castling, Mr Castling.' He paused to find the right words and his hesitancy cost him dearly. The older man launched into the space with damaging effect.

'Dr Fish, when I agreed to help you with setting up this convalescence centre you led me to believe that the young men could return to society, to contribute once more, but that, that thing ... it shouldn't be allowed to suffer like that,' he filled his chest with self-righteous pomp and finished 'where's your humanity man?'

And with that Mr Castling turned on his heel and left the office. He paused at the distraught figure of his daughter sobbing uncontrollably by the front door. The nurse was standing uncomfortably next to her. He gave a curt nod to her and grabbed his daughter's arm. Just outside the chauffeur quickly opened the door of 'The Silver Ghost' Rolls Royce. His pronounced limp is a relic from the battle of Ypres.

With a flourish of exhaust fumes the car drove off. The young nurse stood and watched it disappear up the drive and, in the distance, could see it stop just by the old building that stood just by the entrance of the estate. She was aghast at what she had just witnessed and was unsure about crying out in anguish or anger. Her clenched fists gave no clear indication of what her decision might be.

∽

The chauffeur pulled up to stop at the insistence of the gruff tap on his shoulder from Reginald Castling. He had barely driven half a mile and the car was still chugging out its exhaust fumes.

'You there, stop that at once!' Reginald wound down the window and shouted out. He directed his order at a young lad who was at the top of a small ladder working at a metal sign he was trying to hang, his father had one foot on the lowest step and his only remaining arm was ensuring that the boy didn't fall off.

The sign said 'Haura Hospital, a Convalescence Centre for War Wounded.'

'I'll not pay another penny to that charlatan, so you two can take it down now, now if you please.'

Reginald opened his door and stood upright. His daughter remained seated in the comfort of the back of the Rolls Royce. A handkerchief clutched to her face. He gestured again towards the two men and fully expected his orders to be fulfilled immediately.

The father and son stared back in bafflement. The car was so grand and the voice of its owner so commanding that the boy passed the sign down to his father who awkwardly handled it onto the floor. The chauffeur, having got out of the driver's side, moved to try and help him. The two war veterans allowed a passing smile of recognition showing they understood their shared infirmities.

Reginald stood for just a few moments as though deep in thought. He was staring at the sign with his brow furrowed. Anyone that knew him would know that action would soon follow. Decisive action at that.

He returned to the back of the car and placed his arm protectively around his daughter. The chauffeur hurried back behind the wheel and the Rolls Royce stormed off once more.

∼

Back at the large house the two nurses had gathered in Dr Fish's office. He was pouring himself a stiff drink of whisky and hurriedly drank it down. After his second he looked up and at the two women. He gave a weak smile and beckoned them to sit down.

'Well, that could have gone better.' He rubbed his face and looked very weary.

The older nurse said 'sir, that wasn't your fault, not at all.' She smoothed down her white pinafore and looked him straight in the eye.

'What you are trying to do here is courageous and nothing should stop you, nothing at all.'

She had joined the small private hospital six months ago and whilst the badly burnt and damaged young men had disturbed her at first, she had seen, with her own eyes, the major difference the treatment and experimental surgery had brought about. Some of it is nothing short of miraculous.

The old house was very roomy and they were only using a tiny proportion of it. There were only five patients present and Bob was, by far, the most damaged man they had seen. But she had such trust in Dr Fish, she knew that his work was pioneering and bound to be successful eventually.

'Well, the money from that chap had been crucial, certainly the War Office will not help out if he does stop contributing.' Dr Fish gave another nervous laugh and gestured for the two women to have a drink. Both shook their heads.

'What will happen? Am I allowed to stay?' The younger woman spoke confidently and held herself with a poise and elegance that did not marry with the minor role she had played out at the Front. Not for the first time Dr Fish wondered just why she had been so quick to desert her duties in France and come back with 'dear old Bob.' Her usefulness had been extraordinary and she had learnt and adapted to the needs of the badly burnt pilot with ease and showing a keen intelligence. It had been worth the bribe he had paid to her matron and the pressure he had applied to Reginald.

'I could not afford to lose you,' he replied and immediately felt the quick glare from the older nurse. Sensing that he had missed something but didn't know what, he carried on.

'Neither of you, of course,' he quickly threw out the compliment and noticed the blush from the older woman. Her adoration for him was neither reciprocated nor acknowledged. He merely saw the two women as his assistants. But the younger woman noticed it all and allowed herself a knowing half smile.

He finished the meeting by issuing new instructions about the care needed for the five patients. His line of surgery involved skin grafted from a part of the body not burnt onto the areas that had been damaged, was pioneering and had gained the nickname of 'plastic surgery.'

Bob had been particularly badly injured and his face had no nose, cheeks or lips that anyone could recognise. Just a year ago he would have been dead within a day of sustaining such damage. Dr Fish had been an assistant under Harold Gillies and both had worked at Queens Hospital at Frognal House. But it had been Dr Fish's proposal of using dead men's cartilage that had led to his half dismissal and his subsequent exile to St Thomas's House.

'Right, let's get back to work, let me send a few telegrams. I'll try to sort something out and I'm sure those lads need their dressings changed.' Dr Fish's attempt to bring some order into the disastrous past hour fell very short of the mark. But both women accepted his attempt to be light hearted and left him.

Dr Fish didn't pick up his notepad, nor the telephone. He couldn't face the trials of trying to be connected to the Home Office and knew well enough that, without the support of the influential Reginald Castling, his chances of pursuing his research with actual patients would be very low indeed.

Instead, he lit his pipe and pulled out the photograph of Bob; he then drew out his half-finished drawing and continued to sketch. The main issue would be how to construct a new nose. Within seconds he was deeply in thought and unaware of his surroundings.

~

Martha pulled at the other nurse's arm and they gave a complicit nod to each other. Over a brewing pot of tea they talked over what had just happened.

'It's not fair, he is a genius and should get all the credit he deserves.' Gladys took a deep sip of the strong tea and fiddled with the strainer. She was upset but didn't want the younger woman to see just how much. She pushed against the white dress and tried to adjust her cap, causing one of the bobby pins to come adrift.

The younger woman quickly moved to help her friend and deftly put the pin back, successfully pinning the coiled hair back into place. The towel women, although the age difference was apparent, were quite comfortable in each other's company.

'I've gambled everything coming here too, whilst the offer was too good to refuse, I genuinely thought that Bob needed me.' Martha half spoke to herself as much as to Gladys.

The past two weeks ran through her mind, it had all been a whirlwind. Her time at the field hospital and then her reluctance to leave the badly burnt airman. She had been stunned when the matron had told her that she could accompany him back to England, or Blighty as all the soldiers called it. And when she heard that she would be paid fourteen shillings a week plus full board she had been thrilled. But what she had not told Gladys was that the fact coming to St Thomas's House had been the deal clincher.

Both women tidied the tea things away and returned to work. The other four patients were not as badly damaged as Bob and they could be found in the small common room.

George and Henry were both infantrymen and they had badly damaged faces and, whilst causing them both to hate mirrors, meant that they were able to move. The pair of them were enjoying a slow but competitive game of table tennis.

Alfred, an older man who had a family, sat quietly in one corner, he held a large magnifying glass to his one remaining eye whilst he peered at an old newspaper. His striped pyjamas had rigidly ironed creases and he had the posture of an army man through and through. The last man, Charlie, was practising his walking using his crutches. His face normal on one side and obliterated with scar tissue on the other. He managed four successful steps and his grin of triumph was infectious. The two nurses stood and applauded him.

Charlie turned towards them and shouted with glee.

'I've got the hang of this Miss,' and tried to do a pirouette but tripped and fell. Fortunately he was caught by George who slurred something. His efforts to speak causing spittle to erupt from his mouth.

Gladys had managed to tune in her hearing to understand him and said with a firmness that belied her genuine affection, 'Corporal Wilkins, we do not allow language like that here!' Her voice brooking no disagreement.

All four men stopped and looked expectantly at the two nurses. Their discomfort at their disfigurements meant that they rarely allowed their family to visit and the company of each other and these two women were crucial and all they had.

Gladys took command.

'Right gentlemen, time to go back to your beds in the ward, it's nearly wash time, and then supper.'

The four men groaned and made movements to obey. Their military training and the desire to please Gladys overrode anything else. They could sense that something had happened and the arrival of the Rolls Royce had sparked discussion. But they also knew that they would be told what was afoot, eventually.

'Right Nurse, I cannot wait for tonight's soup,' shouted George as he playfully waved his arm in the air. His patched face with its latticed scars betrayed no emotion as the skin was still healing but his eyes were bright with amusement. It was always soup, they could not cope with solid food yet.

Gladys smiled and followed them out, helping Charlie with his balancing. The soldiers shared one dormitory that cared not for rank nor privilege and it was based just next to the common room.

The other nurse hurried past them and entered a small room next to the front door. Bob was still lying upright in his bed. He was restrained there and the straps went around his chest and pinned him to the large pillow that seemed to engulf his head. He had to be upright to ensure that he could breathe. There were further straps that encircled his head and they were black. The black that was in direct contrast to the vivid red of his face, and any visible part of his body. There was no nose, no mouth that was discernible and his one working eye appeared to have dropped down his face. He was, as usual, moaning in pain and was in a lot of distress.

She hurried over to him and gently took a maimed hand, the solitary finger that protruded from the bandages was at an acute angle.

'Bob, Bob, don't listen to them, I'll stay with you, don't worry, I'm here.'

She knew that he only had a vague awareness that she was there. But she felt convinced that he knew and needed her. Ever since those first terrible hours in France and through the journey and the time at St Thomas's she had tended to him, changed his bandages and helped feed him. She truly believed that Dr Fish would be able to help him. To bring him back to something approaching what he had been.

She finished fussing over him and completed the records that needed updating. Dr Fish had identified some flesh that he felt could be used for the plastic surgery procedure he was convinced was the future. Gillies had developed a Masonic Collar Flap whereby a large flap of skin called a pedicle could be folded into a lube that allowed newly sewn skin to breathe and live. Dr Fish had suggested that this could be enhanced with skin from a donor who had recently died. The doctor also felt that cartilage from another person could be grafted into cavities to replicate destroyed noses.

This practice had been thought unchristian and he had even been entitled a modern-day Frankenstein. His banishment to St Thomas had been his punishment and the little funding he received was inadequate to properly pursue his theories. That is, until a chance encounter with Reginald castling at a cocktail party. A promise of some funding had been grasped by the doctor and he had risked everything by setting up his hospital.

The young nurse held a cup up to Bob's mouth, the lips had been burnt off and an open chasm was in his face. He swallowed the drops of the water as an unconscious thought.

'Bob, you are going to have the first operation tomorrow, it'll go fine, and then more and more.'

She bent forward to ensure that the badly burnt pilot wouldn't splutter, each drop was carefully watched. She finished and checked that the sheets and restraints were firmly in place.

'Nurse, Nurse.'

She turned and saw Dr Fish standing in the doorway. She was barely nineteen years old yet had seen so much horror in France that she appeared older than her years.

'You are so caring with him, you are truly a credit to your profession.'

He paused and added,

'Thank you so much Nurse Griffin.'

9
WEDNESDAY AFTERNOON 23/11/2018

> *'Griffins lack other qualities that other monsters have in mythology: the beaks of eagles aren't very strong, relying on sharpness. Griffons are usually unarmored. Griffons lack any sort of projectile. Griffons tend not to be magical.'* - **Oxford University Press.**

The wallet had proved quite disappointing in terms of cash and cards. Rab had used the contactless debit card successfully three times before discarding it. He knew that the man would probably have contacted the providers by now and was aware of the dangers of overuse.

The driving licence he had kept just in case and he had not used the twenty-five pounds cash yet. He was unsure what the loyalty card meant, it was for a place called Tranquility, and there were five dots filled in out of ten. Rab had kept it anyway.

The bike had proved quite difficult to ride, it was rusty and the gears had seized up long ago. But he had successfully cycled the five miles into the village. Carefully hiding it and his plastic bag in some bushes, Rab made his way into the Cafe.

If the boys had done well at St Thomas's they would sometimes be taken into the cafe in the local village as a reward. Rab had achieved that accolade only twice, but those two times had generated a pleasant memory and Rab settled into his chair whilst awaiting his 'full English.'

There were already four bikers there, the boy thought them silly old men, as they sat with all their leathers on and talked about motorcycles. He gave them very little thought as he considered his options for the night ahead.

'Hey, son. Don't you go to that school up there?'

One of the bikers, his hair too long and grey to merit the young jacket he wore, shouted across to Rab. The others stopped their chat and turned to listen.

'Yeah the one for the naughty kids.' Added his friend.

Rab had a plate of sausages, eggs, bacon and toast put before him. The old lady who worked there gave him a beneficent smile.

'You hush there, you lot!' She turned back to Rab.

'You tuck into this and don't mind them.'

She turned back to the men reprimanding them sharply.

"Leave the boy alone and let him eat, that's a good school up at the old House, my granddaughter works there and they do great things.'

Rab looked up sharply, he hadn't realised that any member of staff lived here, or at least had a connection at the cafe. He looked around again as he carefully wiped the tomato ketchup up with his last piece of toast. The walls had posters of motorbikes and some old pieces of machinery actually fixed to the wall. The thing that always fascinated him was the old pub sign that had been displayed inside after the conversion to a cafe. The wooded background faded now but the image of the griffin still quite clear. Next to it though was the sign that usually hung outside, that of an old Pilot, but, whilst there was a mask over the face, there was only an arm, the other sleeve hung empty.

The woman saw Rab looking at it and remarked 'We are just doing some repairs to the old sign, he'—she jerked her head towards the Pilot— 'once lived around here and had been a World War One Ace.'

Rab eyes opened and he remembered what the social worker had mentioned.

'My School, it was a place for them to get better, wasn't it?'

She nodded and went over to Rab's table, sitting down opposite him.

'Watch out boy, she'll get you doing the washing up soon.' Shouted out one of the bikers and the others joined in laughing. They stood up, gathered their helmets, readying to be off.

'See you next week then Martha, lovely grub.'

Martha gave them a wave and turned her attention back to Rab.

'It's getting on for closing time, are you going to be late? Are you one of the boys that sleeps up there?'

She had a face that looked familiar to Rab somehow, like he had seen her before?

'Nah, I'm not stopping,' Rab hesitated and quickly thought. The school did have some of the boys sleep overnight, there was a separate floor which had up to twelve beds whilst the care staff worked shifts and even slept over too. Rab had never been given the opportunity to stay over and wasn't sure exactly how it all worked. But, he could go and see tonight? Rab let all the thoughts pass quickly and turned towards the cafe owner.

'Don't worry 'bout me Lady, I is going home soon.' Rab glanced around the Formica topped tables and small counter.

'Was this once a Pub then? He beckoned his head towards the griffin. Its claws pawing at an unseen adversary.

The lady formally proffered her hand out. 'If I'm going to tell you my family history I'd best introduce myself.'

Rab smiled and felt himself warming to the old woman even more. She pushed her hand as if to shake.

'Nah, this is the way we do it.' He made a fist out and took her hand, gently bending it into a fist too. The two fists then gently touched.

'And now like this,' he said and made sure his fist hit the top of hers and showed her how to reciprocate, lastly the hands did shake but with the palms pushing against each other with the thumbs pointing.

Martha laughed and made him repeat the process until she got it right.

'Thanks for the lesson, I think that deserves a free cake?'

Rab nodded vehemently, his reversion to a boy happened quickly and he left the tough guy image behind for a while.

Martha gave Rab the whole tour, telling him how her grandmother had run the pub after World War One. They ended up in her small office. Rab's quick assessment showed that she had very little worth stealing.

'I was named after her too, she was once a nurse during the Great War.' Martha continued chatting and Rab learnt that the old lady had lived in the village all her life. She was a widow and had been for thirty years.

Rab, who had been scanning around the room and feeling slightly bored, had casually picked up a framed picture of a smiling boy off the desk.

'He was a lovely boy, back then, not like now.' Martha made the comment without really thinking.

She shook off a memory that she didn't want to share and Martha gently took the faded photograph out of the boy's hand. Rab was suddenly watching the old woman and he felt a jolt of concern for her. He was quite relaxed in her company and still hadn't worked out where he was going to stay that night nor what to do in the future. The only thing he did have planned was to meet Maria the next day, somehow. Of that he was determined.

Martha looked out of one of the windows, the dark November night made it appear pitch black. She shivered and asked, 'Rab, what time are your parents picking you up? Shouldn't you give them a ring? Is your phone OK?'

Rab went even quieter and wasn't sure how to reply, fortunately he spotted another photograph on the sideboard.

'Hey, is that Ms Arnold?'

Martha smiled and rearranged the photos so that the one Rab was referring to had pride of place. Jenny Arnold was beaming from behind the counter in The Pilot.

'Yes, that's one of my grandchildren, she's the one that works up at the old house, you must know her?'

Rab stood up so as to peer at the photograph, pretending to really study it: a pretence just to buy him some thinking time. He turned to the older woman and, trying a full charm offensive, said 'Yeah, I know Ms Arnold, she's one of the best, but surely you is her muvver?'

Martha gave Rab a playful shove and took the photo back off him.

'She only works half a mile away and yet, and yet…'

Rab could see a tear starting to form in the old woman's eye and took a deep breath. He really didn't want her telling Ms Arnold where he was and had realised that there was some kind of rift between the two women. He expected that the police had been told about the bike theft and whilst he wouldn't have minded returning to Hilldowne, he wanted to show Maria the griffins tomorrow.

'Yeah, I need to make a phone call.' He tried to give her a meaningful look and desperately attempted to raise one eyebrow as he had seen in a TV programme.

'Yes, of course you should, I'll show you back to the cafe.'

Briefly, the old woman had regained her composure.

∾

Rab stood just outside the cafe, he cheerfully waved at the old lady who was hovering inside. He pulled the toy mobile phone out of his pocket, one of the things he had been able to buy with the stolen credit card and talked into it very loudly.

"Ello, Ello, yeah, It's Rab, Yeah, I is outside the Pilot – yeah, yeah, OK.'

Pretending to push one of the buttons he then waved at the old woman and signalled that his lift was on its way.

Martha gave a returning wave and carried on wiping down the counter. She had grown lonely over the past few years and the cafe was not making enough money to warrant keeping it going. She turned the OPEN sign over and wandered away. Moving into the office she absentmindedly picked up Jenny's photograph again. There had been something odd about Rab and she couldn't put her finger on it. He had been very attentive as she had told him about Bob the pilot and when she had referred back to the old family story about a mad woman who had lived up at the big house he had been almost still in his concentration.

She smiled to herself, because Rab had been a picture of constant motion, either fidgeting with his obviously cheap ring, or flicking his unruly curly hair. Yet it was that image of his intense look that had caught her attention. She picked up her mobile phone and found Jenny's number. her finger hovered above the keyboard. Should she ring her? After all that had happened?

∼

Rab had seen the old lady go back inside the cafe and quickly ran down the High Street and, checking carefully that no one was watching, found the battered bike and set off once more. It was cold now and the tracksuit, whilst pleasing to the teenage boy, was of a cheap fabric and ill-suited to the winter elements. Cursing at the slow and cumbersome bike he rode clumsily towards the school. Clutching his plastic bag he allowed his mind to run over all that he had just learnt.

∼

Mr Carlyle was very irritated and pulled his reading glasses off his head in vexation. Sighing deeply he picked up the phone and quickly dialled an internal number.

'Good evening, now how can I help you?'

The headteacher was in no need for the usual games and snapped.

'Archie, Archie? If this is Archie, you should not be picking up the phone, but, as you have, go and get Mr Evans for me.'

'Say please.'

Mr Carlyle gave an audible groan and tried to count to five quickly. He knew that Archie was very clearly on the spectrum and politeness was something he treasured. In all likeliness the boy had been directed to answer the phone. No one would have been expecting the headteacher to ring.

'Archie, please could you ask Mr Evans to pop down to my office, if he can.'

The Head leaned back and allowed himself a smile at the situation. It was always imperative to deal with the boys as individuals and know how to approach each one in a way that would work for them. There was no 'one size fits all' approach.

A few minutes later the Head of Care tentatively knocked on the Head's office door and stepped in. He was over sixty with fading grey hair but that was the only indication of his advanced years. He was over six foot tall with big strong hands and an athletic build to his body. Everyone liked him and were always willing to forgive his utter aversion to paperwork because he had real magic when dealing with the boys. The headteacher always described him as 'our very own horse whisperer.'

'Sorry about Archie, he just got to the phone first.'

Mr Carlyle waved him in and beckoned for Mr Green to sit down.

The Head's office was like a magical store, there were pictures and pieces of children's work everywhere, on the walls or in 3D format on shelves. The piles of paper seemed to cover every part of his desk and the Head of Care knew that some of them hadn't been moved for months. Mr Carlyle had once taught History in a mainstream school and there were odd clues around the room to show this. An old and battered World War One poster had been framed and was hanging from a beam that spanned his study. Oddly, he sat facing his whiteboard that had an intricate 'to do' list, his back to an old and tatty desk.

'I was sent an email this morning and have only just been able to read it.'

The Head stood up, he stretched and glanced at his watch. It had a strap with the words 'St Thomas's emblazoned on it.

'Is that the latest thing?' Mr Evans asked, his eyes on the Head's timepiece.

Distracted momentarily, Mr Carlyle nodded enthusiastically and thrust his arm forward so as to show it off. Owen Evans smiled and acknowledged it. The Head was renowned for buying gimmicks which would have the school's name on it.

These would then be given out as spot prizes and rewards to the boys. Often they were also cosseted by staff too.

'Is there one going spare for me?'

'Depends on how you handle this one.' The Head's eyes twinkled and the two men showed how relaxed they were with each other. Both knew 'where the bodies were buried' and whilst they both respected each other's skills, they retained a distance between each other. Owen Evans was always careful to show due deference.

'Owen, I've got to go to a meeting tomorrow about Jethro, apparently he's been playing up and showing worrying behaviour with his foster placement. Anything I need to know about before I go?'

Owen Evans looked surprised. He held up his large hands in a shape expressing both acknowledgement and compliance.

'Nothing at all, he is upstairs right now, been as good as gold.'

'Been swimming tonight?'

The Head of Care knew what was really being asked and quickly replied.

'I was with him myself, all fine, and the risk assessment completed too.'

The Head grunted, understanding that he had made his point and now certain that once Owen had got back upstairs he would ask Anna if she had filled one out. Anna was Owen's second in command and the one he delegated all paperwork to when he could.

'Why, what's been happening?'

The headteacher explained what had been said in the email and, even though both of them had seen most things in their careers working with these sorts of boys, they did share a look of real concern.

The phone rang, both men stopped to listen and once the tone had changed slightly the Head bent over the desk to pick it up. It was an outside line and the small screen showed the number of the AD. The Assistant Director of West Sussex's Children's Services personal mobile was known to very few and used this late even rarer. Mr Carlyle flicked his eyes towards Owen dictating that he should leave.

'Hello Jennifer, to what do I owe this pleasure, you did well to catch me, it's nearly six thirty.'

He had leant back in his comfortable swivel chair and reached for one of the spot prizes, a pen that had an end that could act as a torch. Whilst he listened he flicked the on/off switch, trying to shoot at objects on his desk. His face, initially relaxed and unconcerned, grew grave and, in the end, intensely irritated.

'Yes, yes, of course he can come.'

'Yes, yes, yes, I'll meet him personally and set his mind at rest.'

it was clear that the conversation was not going as it should have. The school had achieved an OUTSTANDING rating at its recent Ofsted inspection, both for the school and its residential facility. An unusual achievement for an establishment with over eighty teenage boys all of whom have behavioural issues. He had thought that he might have some respite from scrutiny, but, he had been told that the LADO would be popping in to have a casual look round and a chat. Also, he would be arriving in thirty minutes!

Rab laboured up towards the start of the drive and hopped off the bike. He had been looking forward to going into the small building there. He wanted to check out the 'Griffins' but it was too cold for that now. He had to find somewhere to shelter first and foremost. Scouting around the outside he could find no obvious way in. It was two storeys high and the windows had been double-glazed. The front door looked redoubtable too. There was some scaffolding up, and part of the outside wall had been demolished but there was definitely no way in that he could see.

Sucking his teeth in frustration, Rab thought hard. His plan had been too simple, he now realised. Going back to his bike, he unhooked the plastic bag he had tied onto the handlebars. The few things he had bought with the debit card were inside and, clutching it tightly, he started down the drive heading for the school.

∽

Simon kicked the ball back towards the tall thin boy who stood in the goal. He played County standard and struck it too well, successfully sending it past the pupil and into the net, again.

'Hey, Simon, always lucky.' Jethro bent down to pick the ball up and rolled it back to the staff member.

'Try once more and then it's my go.'

'Pencil, we will have to go in soon, it's getting too cold and the floodlights are only allowed on for a short while. Remember Mr Carlyle is still here.' Simon pointed at the

BMW that was parked in a marked-out area clearly signposted 'headteacher' near the front entrance.

The boy, who everyone called pencil, as he was so very tall and extremely thin with a badly cut bowl cut, gave a toothy grin and waved his hand to acknowledge the care worker.

The next shot was deliberately stoppable and Jethro easily moved towards it. But, instead of catching it he pulled his leg back and volleyed it with too much force. It rocketed out of the MUGA and landed on top of the row of garages, opposite.

'Oh bugger – sorry Simon, I'm sorry.'

Simon had watched the ball sail over his head and gave a shrug of acceptance. If there was a definition of what to expect of someone who was good natured, Simon would be it. He was rarely, if ever, angry or annoyed.

'No worries Pen, I'll just go and get it, you go on back in.'

Jethro shouted back that he would and moved towards the small entrance through the wire mesh.

'Hey Pencil, Pen, look over here.'

Jethro looked around at the hushed and urgent voice. He saw Rab beckoning towards him from behind a bush near the Multiple Use Gym Area. Pencil gave a warm grin and sauntered over, only realising as he got closer that Rab was frantically holding his finger to his lips and waving over his shoulder. Jethro looked behind him and could see Simon just climbing onto the garage roof. A look of realisation flashed over his features and he hurried over to Rab and quickly hid with him behind the leaves.

'Hey bro, what happening?' Jethro whispered.

Rab kept his finger on his lips and crept away further into the bushes and Jethro followed him. They were soon at the unofficial and designated smoking area. It was at the back of a shed that acted as a tool store for the allotment area. The school had tried to get a qualification going with the Royal Horticultural Society, but the boys had been very reluctant to spend any time digging. But the area acted well as a place to quickly meet and smoke before the staff came out on duty. The floor was festooned with fag butts. Still maintaining silence, Jethro dutifully handed Rab a Rizla and he successfully lit it.

∼

Mr Carlyle came out into the porch of the school and peered out. It was dark but he soon saw the approaching cars' lights. He checked his watch and gave another irritated tut. Then, looking up, he stared in disbelief at the member of staff scrabbling around on the garage roof. He was just about to shout a question when the car pulled up beside him. The old man who stepped out could not have had a job more at odds with its title. He looked nothing like a LADO.

'Mr Sinclair?' Holding out a hand, the Head was unsure whether he should help support him, stand erect or shake his hand.

'Ah, Mr Carlyle.' The LADO eventually stood upright and gave a quick wriggle of his hips.

'Excuse me, my back is particularly bad at the moment.'

He looked at the Head with exceptionally sharp eyes and an inquisitive stance.

'Please, do come in and I'll give you a tour as best as I can in the dark.' Mr Carlyle was keen to get the LADO in before he saw Simon, who was still rooting around on the roof.

∼

The two men stood in the staff room and both had been mentally duelling with each other for the last few minutes. Both had questions they wanted answering but neither would ask them outright.

'Here is our safeguarding board, and you can see, you are recorded and referred to on our list,' the Head pointed, 'LADO, Local Area Designated Officer – see'. He read it carefully and aloud.

But Mr Sinclair's eyes had been drawn to the several large, laminated phrases that were stuck with Blu-Tack above the large whiteboard. Mr Carlyle started to get into his stride. He liked nothing more than to be able to show off the school, his pride and joy.

'Ah, yes, these are our mantras, they are often referred to at the end of the daily morning briefings. Like the sergeant used to do in Hill street blues?'

'Now, I do remember that show, hmm…' The LADO glanced around, he seemed lost in thought and said aloud 'see the wheelchair-

'Fight fire with water.'

'Yes, too often people forget that anyone with SEMH or BESD or whatever label is fashionable, has a special need. If someone is in a wheelchair you don't expect them to walk. So – if some has behavioural issues you cannot expect them to always behave as you would hope.'

IF YOU FAIL TO DREAM. ALL YOU HAVE LEFT ARE NIGHT...

The Head was going to pour out his homilies and it was like watching someone reach for their soap box.

The LADO turned back to the Head and interrupted him before any more explanations would be given.

'Yes, yes, I see, but, if I could just see the boy, in passing, if that's OK?'

The headteacher looked annoyed not to be able to go through each part of the display but acknowledged the request and led his visitor out of the staff room and up towards the second floor where the boarders stayed. He felt confident that the risk assessment would be pristine now, and had not worried about informing Mr Evans of their imminent arrival.

∼

The Head of Care was beside himself with worry, his large hands were almost fighting themselves as he wrung them again and again. He had the propensity to go from being calm and measured to being the best impersonator of Corporal Jones from Dad's Army. he could easily be running around shouting 'don't panic' very loudly.

'What do you mean you left him to come in alone? I don't understand. You had to go on the roof?

Simon had come back into the common room and, not finding Jethro, had searched through the boarding area and casually mentioned Jethro's absence to Mr Green. It hadn't been a major issue to him as the boys were all afforded a modicum of freedom whilst staying over. It was part of their transition training for the outside world. In Simon's brain his actions had been entirely appropriate and right. He, with his benign smile on his lips was going to explain further but it was then that the Head and his visitor appeared.

'Ah, Mr Evans and Simon, may I introduce an unexpected but welcome, nonetheless, visitor, the LADO'. He added for emphasis, 'the County Safeguarding officer.'

Mr Evans mouth dropped open and he frantically tried to sign to the headteacher but was too late.

'Good evening, Simon is it? The old man turned all his attention to the young care worker.

'Did I hear correctly, is Jethro missing?'

∽

'So, how are they hanging Rab.' Jethro took another long drag and handed back the rolled cigarette. He was shivering in the cold evening and wrapped his long arms about his body.

'Not too bad, not too shabby.' Rab felt better for being on the school grounds and Pencil was someone that he gets on with.

'I heard you had been away? Somewhere special?' Jethro asked casually.

'Yeah, I was at Hilldowne.' Rab cupped his hand around the fag end and inhaled deeply. It was nearly finished and they didn't have another.

'Hilldowne.' Jethro said the word slowly and looked away momentarily.

Rab's radar came into play immediately.

'Sounds like you know it, ever been there?'

IF YOU FAIL TO DREAM. ALL YOU HAVE LEFT ARE NIGHT...

Jethro, keeping his face turned away said, a little too quickly.

'Not me Bro, just heard of it.'

Rab was curious now and played an old trick on his friend.

'Yeah, it's all new, brand new, but the bloke who runs it is well old, funny name though, Mr Marmite.'

'Martin?' Said Jethro immediately correcting his friend and instantly regretting it.

'You have been there, hmm, what did you do bro?'
Asked Rab.

Then he fell silent as he remembered that only those needing welfare went there.

'No, don't tell me,' he paused and quickly added, 'Miss Arnold saw me and she told me all about it.' Rab had intended to go on about the building there but Tim's eyes opened as wide as it is possible.

'Ms Arnold Knows? She told you?'

∽

The LADO was fuming, he stood opposite the headteacher in the now empty corridor and looked around to ensure that they were alone. Simon and Mr Evans had gone to check the bedrooms and then the grounds. Two other staff members were doing an impromptu register so that the other eight residents, as the boarders were called, were all present and accounted for.

'Headmaster, am I right that the only boy you have here with a High Court Injunction is missing?' The old man struggled to contain himself. The reports back from Jethro's foster placement had been unsettling and showed that the boy had been showing very odd behaviours for over a month now. Jethro had read the recent newspaper articles about Jon Bond, one of the child killers of Peter Carmichael. There was a growing demand that Bond's new identity be released and for the public to know where he lived and what he looked like now. The article had listed a range of child killers and questioned where they might be now. This had made Jethro very anxious and he had started saying odd things and behaving abnormally.

The LADO gave an ultimatum to the Head.

'I'll give you and your staff ten minutes to find him and, if he doesn't turn up, I'll have to ring the police and tell them about Jethro's real identity and that he is potentially very dangerous.

~

'Really, Rab, that's amazing, I had no idea that she knew. I was always told that only my foster parents and my social worker knew.'

Jethro looked directly at Rab, his face now animated with joy. He liked Rab and wondered if Rab was, also, hiding his true identity.

'What did you do then, why were you in Hilldowne? I thought it was only about drugs.'

Rab looked at his friend and quickly grabbed his throat. His temper exploded and any thought about consequences was quickly forgotten.

'What have yo' heard then Pencil, what do you mean – drugs?'

Jethro pulled Rab's hands off him and fled away. Crashing through the branches and towards the school, his long legs helped him cover the distance in no time. But Rab was running fast too.

'Jethro – Pencil – where are you' Simon had just started shouting out when the boys ran straight into him, nearly knocking him over.

'Simon, Simon, help me, its Rab, he just grabbed me, for no good reason.'

Simon put his arms out and held Jethro by his shoulders, his eyes showed concern and he, as usual, had missed the crucial point.

'Now, has you been smoking? I can smell it on you.' Rab slowly stood up, clearly winded by the collision.

Mr Evans came around the corner and his relief was immense when he saw the boy. But, looking over his shoulder, asked, 'Good evening Rab, young man, and what brings you here so late?'

10

WEDNESDAY 28/11/1918

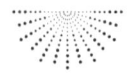

'I had a little bird
Its name was Enza
I opened the window
And in-flu-enza'

— 1918 children's playground rhyme.

'Shhmar, shhmar,'

The Nurse hurried across to the wheelchair; she tried to make her face look cross but it didn't work.

'Yes Bob, I know, I know, I can tell the time too you know!' Martha chided the patient as she fussed over him, tucking in his blanket and checking that his hat covered the one ear that protruded.

'Hey, when is it my turn, come on darlin', I'm always ready and waiting.' Martha deftly slapped the patient's hand before it made contact with her bottom and stood upright.

IF YOU FAIL TO DREAM. ALL YOU HAVE LEFT ARE NIGHT…

'Private Watson, I'll take you for a walk when you've learnt some manners.'

She then wheeled the wicker bath chair out of the crowded corridor and into the cold autumn wind. Bob relaxed a bit and his one good working hand grasped the armrest tightly. He had to lean his head back slightly and away as the cold air might make him cough.

'Right Bob, shall we go further afield today, how about up the drive a little?'

Martha took a firm hold of the handles and set off with a purposeful pace. She needed a bit of time and space as much as Bob and she was going to take full advantage of the opportunity of leaving the hurly burly of the makeshift hospital.

Bob knew that his slurred words would be lost in the wind and he had no power in what little voice he had. It would never carry to the young woman who was manoeuvring him away from the cramped ward and, thankfully, from the prying looks from the other patients.

Bob mused his disfigurement and disability appeared worse, if that was possible, than it was. He had a fragmented memory of those first few months after being shot down and his desire to live had been sorely tested with each operation and every realisation that he was a physical embodiment of a horror show. The hot summer days had seen Dr Fish disappear with the nurse Smith. Martha had told him about their growing affair ever since the funding had been altered. The newer patients had more customary wounds and none were as badly disturbed or damaged as Bob. The Pilot suddenly had a strong memory of himself at that train station back in 1917, he could see himself as he had once been, a slender and handsome young pilot. His memories were brought to an abrupt end as Nurse Griffin sang out,

'Here we are then Captain Courageous, this'll do for our adventure today.' She had stopped at the dishevelled building that stood at the top of the drive. He was wheeled behind a small wall to help protect him from the wind.

'Shhple Shhmar.' He tried to speak again and the intuition that she had developed so successfully since her time nursing him came into play again.

'Good man for being so polite.' She knew that he always started each word with a sound that sounded like 'shh,' and then she just guessed at the rest of the sentence. She reached into her small pocket and retrieved a rolled-up cigarette and a box of matches and quickly lit it, cupping her hand as protection from the sharp early winter wind. She had only started smoking whilst out in France and had found that Bob enjoyed the smell of the tobacco even though he could no longer indulge himself. She did not see the ravages of the fire that had so cruelly burnt him, nor the dramatic results of the efforts to rebuild his face, but only someone that needed her help and kindness. She smiled benevolently down on him and blew the smoke into his upturned face.

Bob's nose had once been part of his knee and whilst Dr Fish had been able to ensure that it worked as a nose, it had no resemblance to one at all except that it was in the middle of his face. The doctor had done impressive work and managed to piece together something that resembled a man, but not a man that could be seen outside a hospital. What made it worse for Bob was that, after the surgeon had left, the soldiers sent to recuperate at St Thomas's had been mainly amputees and minor disfigurements. He was the only relic of the once pioneering plastic surgery work.

Nurse Griffin looked around her and carried on talking. This was their custom, she would talk about the war, the hospital and even herself occasionally, and he would listen and show his understanding by either a look or an attempt at a word.

She glanced around the edge of the small building and turned to change Bob's chair, so he could see the sweeping drive and the large house, now a hospital, at its end.

'There Bob, that's what home looks like from a distance, did you know that it's been around for hundreds of years, that front entrance is original.'

He could see next to the house the sprawling fields and a large farm building that seemed to almost encroach upon the old Manor House. He shuffled around in his seat. His body in constant pain. His wriggling sometimes helped, but only for a short while.

Bob looked at Martha once more and she caught his eye. Nodding, she bent down and released the brake and pulled him out into the path.

'I know that look, yes indeed I do.' She laughed and started to carry on pushing him up past the building and to the start of the driveway. Each day they had gone further afield and he had enjoyed listening to her as they moved. The sheer motion of the wheelchair helped him cope with his uncomfortableness.

'The government have said that the eleventh of November will be remembered each year, everything will stop at the eleventh hour! I wonder if that will happen?' The young nurse had seen too much horror at the Western Front and faced too much personal disappointment to really be optimistic about the future or really trust what the government would do.

'I've heard that women might be allowed to vote now too.' She reached the old road that led down into the village and knew that they could go no further. The villagers were curious about the converted hospital and whilst some of them did work up at the House, the two places did not mix.

'One day we will just waltz straight into that pub.' She stopped and stared at the tavern she could see in the distance and abruptly turned round.

'ShhName?' Bob tried to phrase his question and gave up with but a single word.

'The Griffin,' The nurse answered, then, almost under her breath, 'my family's pub.'

'But not this day.' She gave a little sigh and edged him back up hill. Bending lower so as to gain momentum up the slight incline she didn't see the tree root. A wheel caught on it, crunching loudly and threw Bob forward. With a loud scream he pulled back against the motion and his strap bit into flesh that was still raw. Martha lurched forward and then shouted.

'BOB! BOB!' The distraught nurse struggled to hold the handles which were high and solid. Being forced to release them she felt her shoulder shudder and then lost all feeling in her arm. With a thud she hit the floor and immediately lost consciousness.

'SHHMar, Shhmar,' Bob tried to call out, he could not see the nurse as his one working eye was closest to the ground. All his perspective was distorted and the sharp pain in his remaining leg was dominating his senses.

He pushed against the pain and, by arching his back, was able to shuffle forward and, eventually, move his head to see better. He had been thrown some feet with the bath chair capsizing forward and was now just inches from the wall. He wondered if he could get close enough whether he might be able to push against the wall and then stand upright. His one leg could support his weight when he had a walking stick and it was something that he had been rehearsing for the past week. Bob dragged himself forward another inch or two, each gain costing so much in agony. He focussed on what he had to do, for that moment, nothing else mattered.

Martha came too after a few minutes and just lay in bewilderment on the path. She felt the nausea rise in her mouth. Gently testing her limbs she quickly self-diagnosed a dislocated shoulder. Clutching her elbow and keeping her arms weight high, she was able to slowly bend a knee and pushing down, stand up.

'Bob, Bob, are you alright?' She glanced around apprehensively and could see the upended wheelchair, and, just beyond it, the prone figure of the pilot. She shuddered with pain and a sharp stab of fear. Was he dead?

∽

The nurse negotiated the strewn branches of the tree that had grown against the building. She was panting with the effort of not passing out again, just wanting to reach Bob, but not sure she could in time. She couldn't believe that such a simple mishap could have caused this level of trouble.

Through her tears of effort and pain she noticed that the pilot was actually dragging himself forward, like a giant slug. Each motion is almost imperceptible. She reached the wall and had to sink down against it.

'My God, Bob, are you OK?' She retched as some bile filled her throat.

'Bob, please?'

Bob had heard the nurse and, with an effort showing an amazing level of sheer determination and bloody mindedness, he rolled ever so slightly so that he could face her. He tried to shape his mouth like a smile, and she, able to recognise what he was trying to do, cried out again.

'Bob, what on earth are we doing, how can such a simple trip...' she stopped mid sentence as she was distracted by what he was holding. She slipped down hard against the wall and her dress was touching him. Holding herself awkwardly she turned towards him.

'What on earth have you there? Hmm very odd!'

Martha gestured with her head and Bob bent so as to look at his hand. Somehow he had picked up a slither of masonry, it was definitely made of stone but appeared to be shaped like a small claw.

Martha bent closer to have a proper investigation when...

'ShhMar, shhloo, loo...' Bob, through his pain, was desperately trying to wave his new acquisition towards the wall, just beyond where the nurse was sitting. She slowly turned and peered down. The chair had obviously struck the wall and the claw had become dislodged. She manoeuvred herself even lower and gave a gasp of surprise.

'Bob, I think that thing you've found might fit in this space.' The nurse tried to reach out for it and felt the giddiness descend upon her. She lost consciousness.

'How are you now Captain? I can alter these pillows more if that would help?'

Bob gave a grunt of acknowledgement and managed to shake his head. He did feel better and knew that he should start to respond more politely soon. He had been told that Nurse Griffin had been sent to a local hospital and was being treated for a dislocated shoulder, but that was a week ago now. Bob had tried to find out why she just wasn't being treated at St Thomas's and had only been told that she had developed a cough and had a fever which was making her recuperation harder. He really missed the company and care of the young nurse and wondered whether he could ever cope without her.

~

'Merry Christmas Bob, Merry Christmas.' The young man had managed to negotiate the three yards between the beds and lay his crutches down on Bob's bed. He hoisted himself up onto the chair and his empty trouser legs draped over the edge. He had lost both of them in the last week of the war. Others would see that as the ultimate tragedy but he managed to have an effervescent humour about it all.

'I'm going to get legless today, after all, I'm being fitted with hollow legs soon!'

Bob gave him a welcome nod. Sam Kidd had been his friend and companion over the past month and a good source of any gossip as well. More importantly for Bob, Sam talked so much there was never a need for a reply.

Sam dipped his head conspiratorially and whispered.

'I've got a bottle of the good stuff here,' he tapped his nose. 'My brother left it here last visiting day.'

Bob was thinking about how to show his pleasure when they were interrupted by the arrival of Dr Jones accompanied by Nurse Adams. Their faces were grave and not the usual visage of Christmas jollity.

There were only eight patients left at St Thomas's for the Christmas period. The Manor House had proved impracticable for the servicemen and many had been moved to other accommodation. This meant that the staff had been reduced too.

'Gentlemen, I have some bad news for you all,' the Doctor paused as though lost in thought, and then carried on, 'there is no way of sugar coating this and I'm aware that all of you have faced terrible news over the past year, this can only add to your woes.'

The doctor was talking loudly and not making any eye contact with any of the servicemen all of whom were now listening intently.

'I am so sorry to have to tell you that one of our own, Nurse—'

'SHHNO.' Bob tried to get out of the bed, his flailing arm catching one of the crutches that cluttered onto the floor. Sam managed to catch him and held him tight.

'—Susan Aldridge has succumbed to the terrible flu that has spread around the world. I've had a telegram last night informing me that she has died.'

Bob's head jerked and he tried to speak but only a gurgling sound came out. Sam reached across and held an improvised handkerchief to his mouth and Nurse Adams ran over to the bed: her intervention just saving the two men from falling to the hard floor. Two of the other patients gave loud gasps and one started to weep. Bob, on the other hand only felt immense relief.

∽

Bob was thrilled when Martha walked into the ward, the three remaining patients cheered too. A single, solitary Christmas decoration dangled from the doorway and she had to duck to avoid it.

'Well chaps, I hope you have been behaving yourselves whilst I've been away,'

She was holding her arm a little stiffly, but otherwise appeared to be moving well. She went to each bed and had a small gift for each of the bedridden patients, she explained that they were belated Christmas presents. The last bed she came to was Bob's.

He was feeling such joy and excitement, emotions that he had not experienced for so very long. His speech was better and, with his stick, he was able to make reasonable headway with his walking. His hair grew in tufts and the hairline was very high over one ear but his one good eye was clear and blue.

'Captain, I have to apologise again for that trip. Who would have thought that it would have been that eventful.'

She then lowered her voice and leant in conspiratorially, trying to be casual as she asked, 'do you still have the claw?'

Bob nodded and beckoned with his head to show that it was in his trouser pocket. He had managed to thrust it there just before the ambulance had spotted them stranded by the building. The driver had been en route to the house to pick up a patient and had been astonished to spot the upturned wheelchair and the unconscious nurse. The poor patient had been awake and had been scrabbling around at the base of the wall, but his speech had been unintelligible to the driver. Thankfully, though, the nurses and patient were returned back to the hospital.

Martha gave a smile of thanks. She was pale and the past month had seen her lose even more weight. She looked far older than her tender years.

'I have a lot to talk to you about.' She had a faraway look on her face and obviously had thoughts whirring round her head that she needed to share with Bob.

'Did you know that this place is shutting totally for war veterans?'

Bob gave a small nod. Before Sam had gone, he had shared this nugget of information with the pilot.

'It's a real shame, Dr Fish was doing amazing work and now the place will be turned into a school.' Martha was obviously angry about it and her eyes were blazing.

'Anyway, I've been given permission to take you for that drink I promised you so long ago.' She gave a warm smile and beckoned to the last remaining orderly, who duly trotted over with a wheelchair.

'Don't worry now Bob, I've learnt my lesson, we are getting a lift down there in an ambulance that is leaving in ten minutes.'

IF YOU FAIL TO DREAM. ALL YOU HAVE LEFT ARE NIGHT...

The Griffin's Pub sign swung noisily in the winter wind, and the ambulance driver whistled his appreciation as he drew up outside.

'Darling, I wish I was wetting my whistle with you two rather than taking this miserable sod to Oxford.'

'OY! I bloody heard that!' A short soldier shouted out. He was being moved to another hospital and was well known for his lack of a sense of humour.

It was just before six o'clock in the evening and the pub was open. Martha backed in so as to negotiate the wheelchair into the side bar. The public one next door was already filling up and the keys of the battered piano were being tortured by one of the locals.

'Hello my love, so you've brought him along have you?' The once buxom woman behind the bar hurried round to help them get through the door and into The Snug. There were only two tables and the wall had a solitary poster. Which had a scene of four soldiers firing their rifles from a trench and the large words

WINE WAR TAX

WHAT!

GRUDGE IT FOR US?

NOT LIKELY.

Emblazoned down one side.

Bob could hear a couple of regulars arguing about the score in their darts match and the pianist had started a new song. His harsh vocals could be heard singing:

SIMON THORPE

'GoodBYEE, GoodBYEE, wipe that tear from your eyeE.'

The woman gave a knowing look at Martha and tried to look somewhere over Bob's head as she spoke.

'Pleased to meet you, captain.' She hurriedly wiped her hands on her apron.

'Is that correct, is that the right way to address you?' Bob thought that she was blushing and her cheeks were becoming redder by the second, he gave a slow nod. He looked more closely at the woman and saw Martha's eyes in the woman's face, and the line of the lips looked the same too.

Martha gave a loud laugh at the surprised look she could see on his face. She manoeuvred his chair to make sure that he could see into the bar and then moved round so as to take the older woman's arm.

'Bob, I would like you to meet my old mum, Anne Griffin. Now the sole owner of the griffin Pub.' The two women gave a giggle and Martha tried to courtesy but gave a gasp of pain as her arm and shoulder reminded her of their recent injury.

Mrs Griffin bustled back behind the bar and shouted out, 'Reg, REG! Can you hear me?'

A muffled reply floated back.

'Yes Anne,' mercifully the piano stopped whilst the player replied.

'Reg, you just hold the fort and serve anyone for ten minutes, I'll be in The Snug with my Martha.'

'Right you are Anne, right you are,' came the reply and almost immediately a new tune was being mangled with some words drifting through.

'Hang out your washing on the Siegfried line and cry, cry, cry.'

Anne arrived back at the table carrying a small pewter pot which she carefully put down in front of Bob. She hurried back for two more drinks.

'Captain, there's half a mild in there, is that alright? And we've got a port and lemon each, well why not.'

Bob was very confused and looked expectantly at Martha. She took a deep sip of her drink and this seemed to reinvigorate her. She took up the pewter too and held it up to his mouth. For him to drink was a complicated process that involved directly aiming the fluid at the right angle. But Bob was comfortable with Martha helping him and he gave a hum of delight as he had his first beer for over six months. Anne looked away in embarrassment and started talking to ease the situation.

'Captain, if you could know how much Martha has been talking about you. It's always "Bob can do this now," or "I'll bring Bob down here one of these days."' The landlady stood up and moved over to the poster.

'It was Martha that insisted that we had this made,' she proudly read the bottom of the poster. 'Issued by the Griffin Public House in Haura.'

She turned back to Bob and explained that most pubs had their own propaganda posters, made to show their support for the war effort and in particular, the extra tax on wine. She prattled on about how the Griffin pub had been used to recruit the villagers into the army. The 'Haura Chums' had all joined up together back in September 1914.

'Mum, Bob knows all about that, don't you Bob?'

'Of course you do, dearie.' She stopped and finally looked directly at him.

'My, what you've been through, I've seen some of the boys come back, but I've not seen anyone like you.' She had a questioning look on her face and made to say something but obviously thought better of it.

'So, you were shot down by the Red Baron eh?'

'No Mum, I told you, Bob was trying to shoot the Baron down and was shot by one of the Boche.' Martha emphasised the word Boche and it obviously invoked a strong hatred in her. Something that Bob had not seen her reveal before.

Anne was still nervous and, draining her drink she went behind the bar and started mixing herself another.

'So, was the Baron a redhead then? Or have a red face?' She hurriedly added her lemon and took a deep draught.

'Mum, don't you ever listen properly? I told you, the Baron flew a red plane. He had been told to camouflage his plane and felt that was dishonourable, so he painted it bright red!'

Martha shook her head and beckoned for her mother to sit once more. She gave a look towards Bob which seemed to say 'don't mind her.'

Bob had been watching carefully and tried to make sense of it all. He knew that there was a link somewhere, a reason for this trip but struggled to find it.

Martha took his hand that had suffered the least. She took a deep breath and started to talk. Her story was helped along with interjections from her mother and Reg only had to interrupt twice with questions about serving from the other bar. After an hour Bob was tired and needed to go back to his hospital bed, he also needed time to think through what he had been told. But, the pieces had come together, for him at last.

11
WEDNESDAY EVENING 28/11/2018

'anonymity is an important part of the rehabilitation of children who offend – and naming them as adults, especially in the age of social media 'makes it very difficult for them to put their past behind them.'
- Pippa Goodfellow of the Standing Committee for Youth Justice.

Rab sipped the hot chocolate appreciatively and tried to put his hard face back in position. He hadn't intended to be here, doing this. But his plans rarely turned out as he had thought they would.

'I guess you can't get through to her?'

Mr Carlyle smiled at Rab over the phone. The teenager was sitting in the middle of the small settee in his office and the door was deliberately open. He knew that Mr Evans was within hailing distance in case Rab kicked off. The Head had pursued conciliatory actions as he juggled with the problems that suddenly appeared to have materialised.

'You are right, there is no answer, now, do you have another number, maybe?'

Rab kept a straight face as he replied, 'naw, who'd have two phones, that's just silly.'

Mr Carlyle gave a short 'harrumph' noise and left a message when asked to by the disembodied voice on the phone.

Taking a sip out of his cup, he ruminated aloud, pretending to present the options as if for the first time, although he had already developed a plan, one that he didn't really like, but a solution nonetheless.

'OK Rab, I've contacted the emergency Social Services and they have nowhere for you to go. Mr Stone is happy not to press charges for the old bike you, ha, borrowed? And the wallet?'

The Head cast a look at Rab, who calmly looked back. He continued.

'Hilldowne has suddenly had two cases come in so…'

He allowed the pregnant pause to develop and was vainly waiting for Rab to fill the gap but the teenage boy bent his head and took another drink. His hand had the St Thomas's logo that was emblazoned on it.

'So.' The Head leant back and put his hands on his head. He quite liked the boy before him, his tracksuit looked clean for a change and he had a bright, engaging look about him. Mr Carlyle was aware of the range of issues that Rab grappled with every day. His ADHD and propensity to violence. But he was also aware that Rab suffered from a classic form of ODD.

'Rab, do you know what the letters ODD stand for?' MR Carlyle was going to try a different tack in the hope that honestly would work. It normally did with Rab.

Rab looked coolly back at the headteacher. He had heard all the phone calls and, as usual, had been aware that no one wanted him. It was highly likely that Rab's mother had seen the caller ID and just not wanted to talk to the school. No foster placements, no Hilldowne, just him, and, he concluded, it was him against the world.

The boy had felt bad about grabbing Pencil and could not pinpoint why he had. He wondered if he was all right in the head sometimes. Now he was being asked stupid questions, like they thought he was dim.

'Why, is you saying I is odd then? Different?'

Rab knew that ODD stood for 'Oppositional Defiance Disorder.' He had never liked that particular acronym.

The Head regretted his question and really hoped that the boy would not explode. Particularly as the LADO was still on site. Jethro had been quite upset about the incident and was in a highly charged state anyway. He was in the staff room next door, speaking to the LADO. They also had hot chocolate.

Fight fire with water, the Head reminded himself.

'Rab, that didn't come out well, I'm sorry, what I meant to say is that you can be, sometimes.'

He paused and knew that he was digging a hole for himself. It was only too easy to be lulled into a positive handling situation but he knew that this was not a good time, not at all.

'The behaviour is the behaviour and not the child.' He told himself as well and took his hands off his head, carefully putting them back around the cup. Everything needed to look non-threatening, he needed to tread carefully.

∽

'So, how are you? Recovered now?'

Jethro looked nervous as he sat in the staff room. This was normally a place that no one was allowed in and he wondered if he was in trouble. He had met Mr Sinclair before, at one of his annual reviews. He also knew that one of his foster parents was making her way over to the school and there was going to be a fuss. He hated fusses.

'Why did that boy grab you, does he do that a lot?'

Jethro shook his head and put his long arms around his knees, lowering his head, he started to rock backwards and forwards. The LADO went to put a hand on the boy's shoulder and then thought better of it. Pulling it away sharply. Mr Sinclair was unsure what to do now and felt vulnerable and alone. It was 7.00pm in a school with very few staff in the middle of the countryside. He didn't even have his phone with him.

∽

Mrs Jerome washed her hands with her hand gel for the fourth time.

'Right darling, that's you all finished.' She looked across at the old man struggling to pull his trousers up. She knew that he had arthritis and would take longer than she wanted, but she had had enough right now. Tutting, she went over to him.

'There you are.' She bent low and adjusted the trouser leg, freeing it to be jerked up by the man. He looked anxious to be away too. He grappled with his wallet and pulled out two twenty-pound notes, which he proffered to her.

'Thanks darling, thank you.'

She half helped him leave the flat and tentatively looked outside and down the walkway. The usual groups of young men were gathered at the right places. She couldn't see anything different. Pulling her loose cardigan over her bony shoulders she closed the door and gave a sigh of relief. She reached for her handbag with the intention of giving her sister a ring when she noticed three missed calls from Rab's school and two from that silly social worker. She sat down on the battered sofa and heard the voicemails. Then she replayed them just to make sure that she had heard them correctly.

'Yeah, the silly sod ran away from the foster parents, I Know, I know.' She settled more comfortably and told her sister that she had to go up to the school in the morning. The taxi was due to pick her up at 9.30 and then she could bring Rab home.

'Oh my God no! Sis' I'm so, so sorry,' she exclaimed as she was told that Jason was still in Eastbourne Police station. He had not yet passed anything and was being remanded in custody for a further week.

'Yeah, yeah, I've still got it, yeah.' She listened intently as she could visualise her sisters face at the end of the line. It would be contorted in concentration and worry.

'OK. OK, I'll go and get it and give it to you tomorrow, I promise.'

She walked through to the kitchen as she was finishing the call and reached up to the cardboard tube of smarties that she had bought ready for Christmas. Inside it was a clear plastic bag full of white looking powder. She stared at it for just a second and then carefully shook a small amount out.

∼

Rab gulped down the rest of the drink and nodded towards the old poster.

'I've seen one just like that, today.'

Mr Carlyle grabbed the opportunity and tried to carry on with the distraction.

'Yes, there were two made by the local Pub in the village during the war, this one was for World War Two. He read aloud

'Beer War tax,

What!

Grumble at 1d

For Us?

Not Likely.'

'You see, Rab, each pub was encouraged to make their own propaganda posters.'

Rab looked interested and remarked.

'Yeah, the pub was 'The Griffin', now it's the cafe we go when we is good innit.'

The Head nodded, he knew that Rab was a bright boy but hadn't realised his interest in history.

He gave an unheard sigh of relief and started talking about the war when Rab interrupted him.

'Yeah, but the pilot was actually a real bloke wasn't he?'

Rab had lost his anger for the time being, it really could come on so quickly thought the Head.

'He was a real man, and he was actually in this building for a time, I think he died here, but the records are a bit sketchy. I tried to find out more when I came here. But the school wasn't always a special one, it used to be for privately educated girls and they had cleared out a lot of the old records when it converted'.

Rab gave a cheerful grin at that.

'You mean there were just girls here, not us boys?'

The Head nodded and explained that the girls school had gone bankrupt and the council had bought it off them about eight years ago. He arrived just five years ago.

The boy looked at the Head more quizzically than he had before. He hadn't really thought about the school and its staff much. There were some he liked and many that he didn't, and that was it.

'The Griffin Pub.' He twisted his finger and looked uncomfortable. He was interested but didn't want to engage with the Head. He wanted to stir up the fire inside him once more, to feel as he usually did.

'Nah, forget it, so, I is ODD am I?'

But Mr Carlyle had seen enough to know that Rab wasn't going to explode tonight. He was trying to gear himself up, but the distraction would work.

'Oppositional Defiance Disorder.'

'When I say sit down you have to stand up.' And The Head gave a massive grin and gestured his head towards Rab.

'That's you – recognise yourself?'

Rab couldn't help but grin back. He knew that he could be contrary and allowed the old man to carry on and explain what was going to happen. Rab would stay at the school tonight and that his mother and the social worker would come tomorrow. There would be another meeting, of course, and then a decision made.

'So, do I have to share a bedroom? Coz I don't do that.'

'We've got a single one all lined up for you.'

Rab was really tired and the day had seen him at Hilldowne, the cafe and now at the school. He gave an involuntary yawn and meekly followed the Head out of the office and up the stairs towards the residential area.

∽

Mr Evans had performed his usual trick and the LADO was impressed. Jethro had responded to seeing the old care worker and had come out of his reverie almost as soon as he had heard his distinctive accent.

'Now then Jethro, I think you need a jumper on and then you need to think about getting ready for bed.' The Welshman had sat next to the boy and casually put his arm around the teenager and almost coaxed him to stand up. Nodding at the

LADO, he led the boy out of the staff room and towards the stairs. Both boys saw each other and Rab held up an open-palmed hand.

'Pen, I was out of order, we good, yes?'

Jethro gave a small smile and a bigger nod. Their conciliation was quick and decisive. The two men looked at each other and also acknowledged that the spat was over. Mr Sinclair had come to the doorway and observed everything. He felt that he had learnt more in those last few minutes than he had in a very long time. His relief in the arrival of the head of care to the staff room had come at exactly the right time.

∼

At just after nine o'clock the three men were standing in the porch doorway. Mr Sinclair had regained his composure and was now quite anxious to be away. The Head, though, was reiterating the twenty-minutes-long conversation between the three of them yet again. The Head of Care seemed fine with that and was obviously used to seeing Mr Carlyle's propensity to procrastinate.

'OK then, both lads will stay overnight and I'll stay here too. Owen, I'll have the designated staff bedroom and you'll stay in one of the empty rooms. I think Rab will be fine.'

He then lowered his voice and leant forward, instinctively the two other men followed suit.

'Mrs Wiggins has agreed to come tomorrow with the AD to meet you and me here.' He inclined his head towards the LADO.

Standing straight, he reinforced the action already taken.

'And you have signed the risk assessment?'

Mr Sinclair nodded again, he knew that he was now part of the train of accountability if anything were to happen. But, both boys were safe and the next day could see some decisions being made. He turned to his car and started the engine up. By the time he had reached the end of the drive he was in deep conversation with Jennifer, the AD. He wanted her on board too.

∽

Hours later, quietly crossing the bedroom floor Rab cautiously dipped his head out and checked that the corridor was empty. His room was right next to the staff bedroom and he knew that everyone was probably on high alert. But, he wanted to retrieve the plastic bag with his stuff and check that it was all safe. He had been lent some slippers and pyjamas and it was the first time he had worn anything like that for a long time. Normally he put himself to bed and wore the same T-shirt each night.

There were two security doors that had a push bar to open them. Being as stealthy as he could he prised each one open and propped them with a fire extinguisher against them. The school was really spooky at night and only the emergency lights were on. Rab made his way to the front door and went out into the cold and dark November night.

∽

Jethro followed his friend from a distance and made sure that he was out of sight. He had heard the bedroom door opening and had been curious to see who was wandering about and he hoped it would be Simon on one of his midnight kitchen raids. Jethro was always hungry and would have willingly joined the care worker in demolishing the pudding left from the dinner.

Watching Rab leave the school had piqued Jethro's interest and he peered out. Into the darkness trying to spot where the boy was going. He was amazed when he saw rab reappear with a plastic bag just a few minutes later. A jolt of realisation made Jethro truly shiver, Rab must have retrieved the drugs!

∼

Rab gently pulled at the large oak front door. The keypad required a four digit code. Every boy in the school knew it and when it was changed, the knowledge would spread within half an hour.

Rab was just passing the Head's office door when he had an impetuous idea. He gently tried the door and was thrilled when it opened. Turning on the desk light he quickly glanced around, assessing where he might find what he wanted.

∼

Jethro could not believe what he had just witnessed, Rab must have taken the drugs into Mr Carlyle's office. Questions poured through his head and all the answers seemed impossible. Was Rab planting the drugs to make the Head look bad? Was he making a delivery for Mr Carlyle? Was he collecting more?

The boy felt physically sick with anxiety and his concerns over his own identity made any rational thinking really difficult. He was fed up with attending meetings with all the adults, so many doctors, social workers, child psychologists, psychiatrists. His head seemed to fill with faces, with words. Jethro would be invited in, then asked to leave the room, then asked to explain how he felt and even, when he was younger, asked to do drawings to show his emotions. It felt like he was important but never asked what he wanted. He was really scared about going to prison and had heard, over the years, that this was still a possibility! It was really hard to pretend to be Jethro and he never, ever even said his own name. The only place he had liked was Hilldowne, but that was a few years ago now, before it had been rebuilt.

Jethro stood, totally unsure what to do, he was so sick with worry that his head felt like it would burst. Statue-still, he just stayed in the shadows and allowed the tears to stream down his face. He was living in a nightmare but it felt like reality.

∾

Rab gleefully put one of the mugs into his bag and toyed with the pen torch. It was already starting to bulge with the St Thomas's goodies and he knew that Maria would be pleased. He stopped to look again at the poster showing that 'The Griffin Public House' had copyright ownership. He nodded to himself and wondered about taking it down and giving it to Mrs Arnold down at The Pilot. Gently taking it off the wall he was shocked to see the safe.

Rab was mesmerised and looked in wonder at it. The safe looked just like one in an old Western film he had seen once. That one had been blown up with dynamite. He gingerly turned the protruding handle and was further shocked to feel the door give.

Glancing behind him and checking that he could not hear anything from the corridor outside he pulled the door fully open. Using one of the pen torches he shone a bright light in.

∼

Jethro suddenly let out a piercing scream, and just would not let up. Almost gasping for breath he seemed to be dancing on the spot, with his arms and legs flailing in perpetual motion. He didn't notice the strong arms holding him nor that he was manually carried into the Head's office. It was only after a few minutes that he could hear the reassuring voice of Owen Evans.

'Jethro, Jethro, I want to let go of you, can you hear me, can I let you go? Can I? Can I? You are better than this, trust me, trust me.'

The Head of Care's placating tones and soothing choice of words started to penetrate Jethro's mind and he soon became aware of his surroundings.

'There, there, young fellow. Crikey, what's happened here, some sleepwalking is it?' Jethro blinked and tried to focus on the old man.

Owen had set his phone alarm at two-hour intervals so that he could do a round of checking on the boys. There was no payment for waking staff and anyone sleeping in should expect to do just that, but Mr Evans had been aware of the exceptional circumstances and taken the necessary control measures as laid out in the risk assessment. He had noticed Jethro's door was open and quietly followed the tell-tale tracks of the propped-open fire doors.

The two of them were sitting on the small settee. Rab was rammed underneath them. He could not believe that this had happened to him for a second time and was determined not to bite on anything! Instead he clutched his plastic bag and could do little else but listen. Very gently, he pushed the small cardboard box with his feet and made just a little more room for himself.

Jethro was still shaking, he felt as though his whole world was about to disentangle. Babbling aloud he heard himself say the random thoughts that were in his head.

'The Head's on drugs, I knew it, I knew it.'

'But, I didn't mean to hurt her, no, not never.'

The boy looked imploringly at the Head of Care and, slowly, but surely, let his tongue stop its conversion of thoughts to words said aloud.

Mr Evans just let Jethro settle. He didn't judge nor show his reactions to what he heard from the boys under his care. He had an ability to acknowledge the bad but always see the good. Within just a few minutes Jethro had regained his composure and wanted nothing more than just to go back to bed. He assumed that Rab must have left somehow and he had no intention of telling the member of staff about the drugs, nor that Rab had been wandering around at night. Rab could be quite scary, but was, also, one of them. Rab's business is Rab's business, he thought to himself.

Mr Evans guided Jethro out of the office and, talking more to himself than to Jethro, he wondered how the boy had managed to move the fire extinguishers whilst sleepwalking.

∼

Rab moved quickly as soon as Jethro and Mr Evans had left the office. He had been fortunate that neither had seen the poster off the wall which he now hurriedly put back up. Pushing the settee back into place his foot caught the small cardboard box that he had moved. Glancing down he noticed it said on the side, 'Stuff from the old desk.' For no other reason than mere curiosity he looked inside and, not quite believing his eyes, saw a small stone claw. He grabbed and thrust it into his plastic bag and hurried up to his room. Fortunately Jethro had convinced the old man that he needed a drink and the two of them had gone to the residential kitchen. Rab had just enough time to get to his room and throw the sheets over himself. Just a few minutes later he heard the door softly open and knew that Mr Evans was checking on him. Successfully making some sleep-like noises, Rab laid as prone as he could. As soon as the old man had closed the door Rab took out his pen torch and surveyed his treasures.

He had a St Thomas's. Lanyard, pen torch, mug, ruler and, he thought hard for a second and struggled with the word, a karabiner. Then rummaging through the bag, he pulled out the seat of keys that had been in the safe. He grinned as he saw that one Yale key had the word 'Master' on it. Extremely pleased with his evening's work he turned to go to sleep and felt the stone claw sticking into him. Jolting upright he looked more closely at it. Could it be a claw of a griffin he wondered?

12
WEDNESDAY 5TH DECEMBER 2018

'Griffins are known for guarding treasure and priceless possessions.' - **Irene Lambert. (fantasy author)**

Bob heard the midnight chimes and pulled at the strap above his head. Carefully hoisting himself upright he swung his good leg over and gently stood up, holding the side of the bed for support. Reaching out, he gratefully grabbed the adapted walking stick by the side of the chair. Leaning heavily on his working arm he managed to negotiate himself out of the small ward and into the corridor. All was quiet and he carried on, out of the front door and into the cold wintry night.

Shivering and tired from the short distance he had successfully traversed, he rested for a couple of minutes. He tried to wrap a scarf around his face to help protect his ravaged face from the elements and he fitfully tugged at it, hoping to make it more secure. Looking around for anywhere to sit down he seriously contemplated giving up on his venture and returning to his warm bed.

In his mind he smiled and became the man he truly was, courageous and inquisitive. He had listened to Martha and her mother and was due to meet with them later that day. But, first, he wanted to find out something for himself.

Bob took over half an hour to get to the small shed that was only one hundred yards away. Fortunately the adapted soap box was still there, with the small, oddly shaped paddle nearby. It had been the brainchild of Sam's before he had left and Bob knew that it did work, after a fashion. Lowering himself onto it he pushed against the ground and felt the self-made go-kart move away, gathering a little bit of pace as it went, thankfully, downhill.

The night was well lit by a remarkably bright moon and the badly burnt pilot with a disfigured face with only one functioning arm and leg slowly made his way down the long drive and towards the building that held a secret. One that he wanted to check out himself. Each push against the part gravel and part earth drive was hard and the yards won were gained by sheer determination and a bloody mindedness that had always been part of him. To make the grind easier he ran over what the women had told him the previous night at the pub.

'So Bob, this is where I was brought up,' Martha had gesticulated with her arm and spun around, her head, encompassing the small snug.

'When the Haura Chums all signed up, all on the same day, with Sir Charles from the big house leading them, well, we all cheered. I was only fourteen and so proud of my two brothers in their smart uniforms.'

Anne had stifled a sob at that point and Bob saw her looking at a photograph on the sideboard, one that he had not spotted before. It showed a line of soldiers marching past the pub, their faces grinning as though on a great adventure as they passed The Griffin.

'Like so many villages and towns all the lads joined up together and...' Martha had paused, looking at her mother for support but none was forthcoming, Anne was reliving her own nightmare.

'...Well, you know what happened, it was Passchendaele for those lovely smiling boys. A Massacre – out of thirty that left only four came back. Only four! Not my brothers Billy and Joe, not my sweetheart Frank, no, not them.'

Anne seemed to awake from her reverie, she spoke as though in a dream and had looked at the pilot, whose expression was impossible to read through his damaged face.

'The silly boys had lied about their ages, they were only seventeen, my darling twin boys.'

∼

Bob had to stop, his arm was aching and many of his stomach muscles had been damaged when he had been burnt. He knew that he had to rest but the building was only fifty yards away. He didn't know how long he had been paddling but he could see the prize. Reaching into his pocket of his dressing gown he pulled out the small bottle of whisky that Sam had given him before leaving. Awkwardly biting at the cork with a side tooth he pulled it away and poured a large sharp gush of the golden liquor down his throat. Gagging more than was wise he poured yet more and felt the burn in his stomach. He felt good and bad in equal measure.

Right you daft bugger, you've come this far, might as well finish the job, he thought to himself and set off once more.

∼

Martha had told Bob about her father and the pub. She had explained that the pub had been owned by the Griffins for over a hundred years and that the family had lived in the area for a really, really long time. Anne had added some detail about how she had met Bill Griffin at a market day and fallen in love with the tall and handsome farm boy. How his brother had died suddenly and that it had fallen to Bill to take over the pub. She looked proud of her memory and spoke about the twins and Martha. But Martha had not shared her warming recollections and had been impatient to add to the family story. Bob had been told so much that he struggled to put the chronology in the right order.

But it was clear that Bill had changed to a monster practically overnight after the death of his sons. His drinking became excessive and he was violent towards his wife and daughter. But it had all come to a head when he had come home earlier after helping at one of the local farms. The pub has been left in the capable hands of Anne.

'I had only asked Fred upstairs to say goodbye to him. I'd known him all my life and now he had been called up. He was going to France to die, I was convinced of it. He would not come back, just like my brothers and, and … like Frank.'

Martha had given out such a sob that Bob had longed to reach out to her, to hold her and say that he understood. But all that he had been able to do was sit and listen. Anne had finished that part of the story.

'Honestly, Bill was a different man, he had become so violent and angry. So angry!' Anne was obviously reliving that afternoon, just a year ago.

'Well, Bill had come in and I'd not heard him, he just went upstairs and heard Martha – you know – well, I couldn't blame them, not after all the heartache the whole village had endured.'

Anne gave her daughter a wistful smile. Looking directly at her she said, 'honestly, there was nothing wrong in it, not then.'

Martha had recovered part of her composure and had continued.

'But Mum, the words he shouted at me, calling me a whore, saying that he had no daughter, that he had no children anymore.'

Anne stood up and went to Martha, gently stroking her hair. Both women had a shared memory that brought no happy recollections, a nightmare that would probably visit them regularly before they died.

Gulping noisily, Martha finished her story. She rushed her words as though just wanting to finish the horrible episode. Bob learnt that her father had chased them out of the pub, even causing some neighbours to come and stare. Martha just didn't come back and had joined the QAIMNS. Bob was only too familiar with the nurses from the Queen Alexander Imperial Military Nursing Service. She had smiled at him then.

'And then I met you, so brave and so, very badly hurt.'

Anne then took up the story.

'But Martha had written to me and I kept her letters secret, Bill never knew how brave our darling daughter was, he just sunk more and more into his bullying and drinking ways.'

Martha, gulping back her tears, further explained that the opportunity to come and work with Dr Fish at the 'Big House' as she called it and, possibly, be able to see her Mother again was too good an opportunity to miss.

⁓

Pushing hard against the walking stick Bob made his way right up to the wall. Dawn was starting to break and he knew that his absence must have been noticed back at the hospital, or should he say 'the Big House' he wryly wondered. Hoping that the branches were obscuring him from view he leant against the wall and allowed his body to drop down.

He was shivering badly now and felt as though his body was on fire at the same time. Perhaps Enza had flown in for him too, he wondered. Embracing death, here and now, after all that he had been through, now wouldn't that be daft he thought.

The sliver of stone looked almost magical as he held it up. It was only about four inches long but was clearly shaped like a claw. Grunting with effort he rolled himself and managed to face that part of the wall he remembered from the day of the fateful 'trip'. There it was, he thought, peering down with difficulty he pushed his face closer and made out a clear space, just like a slot. As though working in slow motion he brought his mangled hand up.

He inserted the claw, initially struggling with it and was rather astonished to feel the masonry almost click, just like a lock being opened with a key. He gently pulled back and the claw came out but also pulling a stone box. Bob dragged it back and felt a pang of excitement. The end of the claw protruded out slightly and the box appeared to have something in it.

∽

The hour had passed so quickly in the pub and the mother and daughter had brought such tension and mystery to the proceedings that Bob had felt quite bewildered. But the women had saved the best until last. Whilst Martha had been 'up at the House' her father had fallen ill and died, another casualty from the Spanish Influenza. Martha had actually gone back to the Pub to recuperate from her dislocated shoulder.

But, it was when the two of them had gone through Bill Griffin's documents that they had found an old family Bible. It had been almost discarded amongst the pile of papers found in the bureau.

'Paperwork was never Bill's strong point and my reading and writing isn't all that either,' Anne had explained.

'The thing is, Bob, the amazing thing is.' The two of them had given each other a look.

'Just inside the cover there was a record of the family.'

'Yes,' interrupted Anne.

'The family tree went back over four hundred years – imagine!'

Martha smoothed down her dress, it was only then that Bob realised both women were still wearing black. He had trouble adjusting to the days let alone the weeks since his injuries.

'There was a diagram, a drawing of a griffin and a phrase,'

'Well, would you like to see it?'

Bob was perplexed as to why they were being so open with him. What could he do to help?'

Anne went behind the bar and quickly returned with a small leather-bound book, it looked old and she held it reverentially. Bob remembered that his old grandfather had kept one too. A sudden jolt coursed through his body. Not one of his family had visited him and he had felt rejected by them as much as his fiancé.

His memories faded back to reality as the book was held in front of them.

'Do you see what we mean?'

∼

Bob almost dropped the vellum-bound book. It was surprisingly heavy and took him by surprise. Surely this was not what the women had meant? He tried to bend his head so that his good eye could see into the stone box. Struggling and in some discomfort he pushed his working hand into the chasm. His three fingers were lacking flexibility due to the scarring from his burns and he gave up his search quite quickly. He assumed that he had found the prize with the book.

'Captain, captain, are you up there?' Shouted one of the orderlies. His voice sounding quite close by.

'Look, there's that old soap box Sam had made. 'Nurse Adams gave a shriek of pleasure at her find.

'Bob, Bob, are you up here?'

But Bob, tired and almost rigid with the cold, had fallen prone once more. His fight against all that happened to him over the past six months had taken a massive toll. His last effort had been to push the stone box back and turn the strange key. As he had pulled the claw out he had fallen into a comatose state.

'Here he is, I can see him!' The nurse ran up to the prostrate figure and tried to set him upright. But she needed help as the pilot was drifting into a world of his own.

He could see the sun glinting off the propellers and feel the wind buffeting the plane. He knew that he had to do something before he let go. He vaguely felt his fingers holding something, but it all seemed unimportant. He was dead before they could get home back to St Thomas's.

∽

Dr Carter was more than a little angry. He was standing behind his desk with his hands behind his back, a sure sign that he was not going to break any interruptions nor disagreement. The two women sat in their chairs opposite him.

Nurse Griffin and Mrs Griffin, I cannot believe that you two can have the effrontery to come here and be so demanding, it really is quite ridiculous and beyond anything that I have ever experienced.'

He had been called out to see the dead body and had signed the death certificate with the catch-all diagnosis that most medical practitioners were using in early 1919, that of Spanish flu. It was clear that Bob had been out in the type of weather his constitution could not possibly cope with, and he had been showing some symptoms beforehand too. His meagre possessions had yielded up very little in terms of substance. A signet ring that he had been unable to wear after his injuries, some letters and an old, battered suitcase with clothes that were not suitable for the man he had become. The only items that had appeared at odds with what might be expected were a small book wrapped in an oiled cloth and an oddly shaped stone claw. Those two items were on the desk in front of the doctor.

Martha had bloodshot eyes and the death of Bob had clearly distressed her considerably. The Doctor had been impressed with her nursing skills and had afforded her a modicum of trust for some months. But the incident when she had taken Bob up to the old building at the end of the drive, when both of them had been injured as well as a valuable hospital wheelchair damaged coupled with her taking him to the local pub, had destroyed the respect she had forged.

'I have allowed you two more time than I should have and this nonsense will end now. Nurse Griffin, you are formally dismissed from service and I will be recommending that you are never employed as a nurse again. You know that the House has been bought by a private girls school and thus everyone is leaving anyway. But it is a great shame that you will get no references from me for whatever employment you shall seek.'

The older woman also appeared upset, she was not crying he noticed but just seemed to be broken. Neither had offered

IF YOU FAIL TO DREAM. ALL YOU HAVE LEFT ARE NIGHT...

any real resistance to his phlegm.

'To suggest that either of these things should be given to you two, you, you…' He struggled to find a noun that conjured up what he thought of them.

'…Well, words fail me, I think it is high time that you left.'

∽

As he watched the mother and daughter trudge up the drive and having checked that they had safely gone a fair distance, he went back to his desk and held up the bound book with glee. Fingering it with extreme care he wondered aloud just how much an original book by Thomas More would fetch in the antiquities market. Giving a wide smile of anticipated wealth he searched around and found his personal briefcase. Carefully rewrapping the book, he packed it away and gently tapped the outside of it.

After just a few moments of daydreaming he awoke from his trance and went back to his desk. The mound of papers and documents that festooned it told their own tale of the administration yet to be performed to effectively end the role of the House as a hospital. His appointment had been a last-minute holding exercise anyway and he had hoped to retire soon. Tutting, he reached for his pen and, without a second thought, tucked the stone claw into the top drawer of the large desk.

∽

Martha was marching around the snug whilst her mother was reaching for and pouring the much-needed port and lemon, one for each of them.

'My God, poor Bob, oh God, oh God, Oh God.'

She clutched at her chest and paced with increasing intensity. Her eyes were ablaze and she was both angry and upset.

'Martha, please, it's not your fault, the poor chap was only half a man as it was, and you told me that he was in pain daily.'

'Mum, I know, I know.' Finally, Martha stopped at the bar and took a long sip of the strong alcohol. She was still, technically, a teenager and the burden of being a strong adult had been catching up with her for some time. She gave her mother a despairing look and Anne responded quickly and decisively. She came round the bar and gave her daughter a long and loving hug. She held Martha at arm's length for a moment and gave a sigh.

'My darling girl. I am so proud of you and you've done so much.'

Martha tried to smile through her tears and wiped her nose clumsily with the back of her hand.

'Losing your brothers, losing your childhood friends, losing Bob – it's all too much, what we need is a change, a real change!'

Martha nodded and drank the rest of her glass.

'What shall we do then Mum.'

'Well, at last we know that the Griffin treasure was just an old book, that silly doctor is welcome to it. How about we change the name of the pub? It's about time we dreamed again and stopped living in this nightmare.'

13
THURSDAY 24TH NOVEMBER 2018

'People who enjoy meetings should not be in charge of ANYTHING' — **Thomas Sowell**

'I'm really shocked that you hadn't told me before, really, really upset.'

The Head looked across at Jessie Jones, his deputy, and thought to himself that she had a face like a 'slapped arse' most of the time but today the vivid red in her cheeks looked ready to explode with pent up anger and resentment.

'Just like a chocolate teapot.' He summed up his view of her professional skills before continuing.

'Jessie, a High Court injunction is exactly that, only those listed are allowed to know.'

He gave a meaningful look at Owen and slowly the Head of Care's grizzled features altered into a semblance of comprehension and he took the proffered prompt.

'Crikey, you should have told me at least!' Mr Evans lied badly and no one at the Head's meeting believed him.

Each morning the Senior Leadership team met at 8.30 to have a quick catch up and prepare for the full staff briefing at 8.45. There were five of them crammed into the office and preparations had already been under way for Christmas. This sudden sharing of information about Jethro was only new news to Jessie. The HLTA or Higher Learning Teaching Assistant, commonly known as Little Jo was privy to most information as her ability to keep a secret had been tried and tested with remarkable success on more than one occasion. The assistant headteacher, or Big Jo was taking up the whole settee and had his laptop perched on his knee. He, also, had been told about Jethro some time ago.

'OK, I'll mention that the conference room is busy and the AD is in just to see you about general matters. Shall I say that she might have a tour as well?' Big Jo was being pragmatic and practical as usual.

Mr Carlyle nodded, it always helped for staff to be on their toes, the approach to the end of term was always tricky and too often everyone would start with too early use of videos and quizzes. The idea of someone from the County being around would sharpen up everyone's practice.

Little Jo, normally quiet and agreeable inclined her head too, and, in her mind, was already dishing out jobs to her TAs involving tidying noticeboards and ensuring key words were adequately displayed. With the briefing finished, Big Jo sent it off as an email to all staff so that those on duty could reread it later and slowly managed to extricate himself out of the settee which gave a groan of respite.

'That's the chair – not wind,' he said. But no one laughed as he said the same joke most mornings. The Head of Care and the Head then made their way out into the cold late November wind. They enjoyed helping to greet the boys as they arrived in their taxis whilst the Deputy and Assistant Head went into the staff room next door to deliver the briefing. Once Little Jo opened the door the packed room burst into applause.

'Oi, Oi, here they come.' Smithy led the clapping and his booming voice drowned out all the conversations. Big Jo negotiated his large frame through the scattered chairs and settled in front of the whiteboard which was smothered in timetable cover, instructions, information and even requests for the prompt payment of coffee money. Its spidery writings in a mass of colour. The day at St Thomas's had begun.

∼

'Look, Ian needs to be isolated today, that's two staff, rotating, and then we are light at the break. Not everyone can have a TA today, you can see we have four off ill and the Head is really keen for the reward trip for Year Nine to go out.'

Big Jo was popular amongst the staff yet even he was struggling, the term had been a long one and there had been five restraints the previous day with one member of staff being hurt. But this had resulted in only one fixed-term exclusion and two sets of isolation. He was being pinioned back by questions that were becoming more and more assertive.

'Look, ladies and gentlemen.' He pointed towards the large clock which was showing that it was nine o'clock, there were no bells at this school, staff were just trusted to keep to the timings.

'So, have an extraordinarily pleasant Thursday, remember to complete your log sheets and—'

He paused and looked at the range of mantras stuck to the wall

'—Remember, WE HAVE NOTHING TO FEAR BUT FEAR ITSELF.'

As the staff streamed out of the haven of their room the shouts and bumping noises of another restraint could be heard by the student entrance. Some staff turned and hurried away, others went to help, either by redirecting some of the boys who wanted to stand and watch, or by being involved. After ten minutes the Head was bathed in sweat and worried about the impending arrival of Jennifer, the AD. Thoughts about Rab had gone, the meeting with Mrs Jerome had already been delegated to Jennie, his deputy.

∼

Rab wanted to see the restraint at close quarters, he felt quite emotional when he watched them and always wanted to go and help the boy involved. Yet he felt better for knowing that no one could just do was they wanted, he liked it that there were rules with consequences, even though he pushed against them.

'Move along lads, nothing to see here, move along.' Rab felt the push from Smithy's large stomach as it accidentally caught him.

'Ah, young Rab, nice to see you back.' Smithy's booming voice dominated the small area and, now, everyone knew that Rab was back. Rab noticed that both Mr Evans and Mr Carlyle were involved in holding Ian down. He hated both men for past occasions like the one he was witnessing, but the hate was something that he purposefully fuelled rather than one that was natural. He had to resent anyone who held onto him, who stopped him even though he needed that brake, he needed to know that someone cared enough to actually stop him tearing down everything and hurting anyone in his way.

'I'm fully glazed now Rab, want to collect it after school?'

Rab nodded, his thoughts being reverted back to today and the prospect of collecting his artwork made him smile. He made his way over to the changing rooms. There weren't enough staff to put him in isolation and he knew that his mum and that social worker wouldn't be here for ages. But, due to the staff shortages, Year Eight and those left from Year Nine who had not been allowed out on their trip had to join together. Luckily the lesson was PE.

'Pen, Pen, what was you doing last night?' Rab whispered to Jethro as the two of them got changed. The tall boy looked uneasy and glanced at him.

'Rab, I saw you, I saw you—' He gulped nervously and quickly rethought what he had been going to say. He had remembered what Rab had done to him last night when he had mentioned drugs.

Rab gave an easy smile, he had believed what he had heard and had assumed that Jethro had been sleepwalking. Unaware of the range of possibilities that the other boy had been thinking, Rab carried on, carelessly.

'I got a really good stash out of the Head's office, wanna see it?' He gestured with his head back over to where the boys had hidden last night. Rab had replaced the plastic bag there early this morning and was looking forward to seeing Maria's face later that day. How he was going to get to Hailsham to meet her was a problem that he hadn't worked out yet.

Pencil shook his head violently and quickly left the changing room. He ran over towards the MUGA and started to relax. He hoped the football game would make all his worries disappear.

∽

Big Tim printed off the risk assessment and passed it to Carole to check over. She scanned it quickly and signed at the bottom.

'Well done big man, I'll just get the Boss to countersign it and we can be off.'

She was looking forward to the short excursion out and, even though the weather was cold and miserable, it was good to get out of the feeling of enclosure Hilldowne generated.

'Just one quick signature and then Tim and I'll be off with Maria, the appointment is for 11.30 and we should be back for 1.30.' She had started to speak as soon as she opened Mr Martin's door and was taken aback at his raised hand.

'Oh, right, thanks, hmmm – all's well that ends well I guess. Rab could have come back here last night at a push and I'm disappointed that my deputy had given you, well, hmm, let's call it misinformation.'

The manager of the Home quickly finished his conversation with Mr Carlyle and beckoned Carole to take a seat. Taking the proffered document, he added his own signature and checked with her about the arrangements.

'Right Maria, let's go and get in the car then.' Tim shouldered the small first aid kit. The two staff members escorted the small thin girl out of the common room, through the airlock and into the courtyard. They were using Carole's own car and headed off towards Hailsham.

Maria had a small rucksack with her too and had secreted all the money she had in the world – £4.55. She had also packed a tiny sachet of perfume that she had been given last Christmas. It had come from a Groupon Advent calendar and was the only gift from her mother. She was really excited about the visit even though she dreaded what the dentist might say. She had absolute trust that Rab would be waiting for her.

~

"Ello Darlin' ain't you lookin' pretty then?'

Eric had loomed up and was standing next to the taxi. Asif looked apprehensive and more than a little sorry for himself.

Eric leered at Rab's mother and made her grab one of her breasts as she approached the car. But she was too fast for him and neatly ducked his clumsy grope.

'Hi Eric, fancy seeing one of the Blokes this early in the morning?' She tried to make a bright and breezy remark and made it as if to open the car door. Eric, having been made to look foolish by her quick movement, made sure that his ample bulk filed the space.

'Asif, a moment ... NOW!'

The taxi driver looked relieved to be sent away and, as soon as Eric shouted, he moved, not looking back.

'Right, you little scrubber, you know you owe. You and that fat cow of a sister. You know!'

He had leant so low that his head was almost resting on hers. She could smell the kebab he had eaten the previous night and his hoody stank of his cheap and sickly deodorant. She shuddered as she felt his chubby hand half caress her head and ear with the fingers suddenly twisting her lode violently.

He made her head nod, again and again. She gulped and tried to be calm as she said 'darling, I know nuffin, the stupid idiot must have had 'is own.'

She tried to think quickly and cleverly but had merely said the wrong thing at the wrong time. The story of her life really.

'Had his own eh?' Eric loosened his hold on her ear.

'I'd best have a word with your boy, hadn't I.'

'No, no, I didn't mean that, he hasn't any, God no, I don't know!'

There was a release of pain but she could still felt the sensation of his fingers on her hair and ear. She felt nauseous, sick with worry for Rab and a strong repulsion for Eric and all the 'Blokes.'

Quickly opening the car she was relieved to see that Asif was already behind the driving wheel. He started the car and she looked behind her. Eric was already speaking into his phone.

∼

Rab was on form and had scored an easy hat-trick of quality goals. He was in his own world, one where he was adored by the large crowd and each of his tricks and sleights of skill was applauded and appreciated. The cold November wind was irrelevant and his problems were not in his mind at all.

'Right lads, that's it now, everyone in.' Little Jo shouted out and beckoned that the match was over. She had a small umbrella and was unfurling it. Rab was suddenly and only too well aware of his surroundings.

'Rab, ain't that your mum over there?'

Rab turned at the information and his shoulders tightened with tension. His mother was just getting out of the taxi, her one good coat wrapped tightly and her too high boots elevating her.

'Yeah man, now the fun begins.'

Rab was immediately and totally full of anger. His constant embarrassment at his mother coupled with a genuine desire to go and speak to her, to check that she was all right? Had the Blokes been round to her? Was Jason OK? There were too many questions and each one made him more and more uptight. He could feel his face flushing and beads of sweat were forming on his forehead.

'Boys, boys, I've got to trust all of you will have a shower.' Little Jo and another TA called Fi were standing by the changing room door and were only too aware that no one would be washing, let alone showering. The success criteria for the last half an hour had been to merely to keep the boys occupied whilst the cover for all the lessons was being readjusted. Ian's restraint had led to crucial paperwork being completed and the knock-on effect was rippling through the timetable.

'What's happening at the break then? There will only be four of us on, surely the care staff will have to help?' Fi looked plaintively at Little Jo and the small woman grimaced in a reply. She liked Fi but found that the younger woman was unsuited to the emotional rigours of working in such a school. She got too angry at some of the poor behaviour rather than just seeing it as an interlude between the boys being really just like any other child.

'Fi, you keep an eye on Jethro, just watch him no matter what and I'll have a walk round the grounds near the MUGA.'

'Really, Jethro? He's fine, why does he need special attention?'

Little Jo mentally bit her tongue, Fi was quite right, it made no sense to prioritise Jethro like that, but she could not explain to her colleague. Yet the older woman had a feeling that the break ahead would be difficult and that the Jethro problem might reveal itself, in some way. She nearly changed her mind when she saw the cavalry coming out of the front entrance. She sighed with relief at the large and amiable figure of Owen Evans. She hurried over to him.

~

Mr Sinclair had met Jennifer as directed in the main staff car park and the pairing of them were busy conferring as another car pulled up. A harassed middle-aged woman quickly gathered some papers and joined the two of them. She was an experienced foster parent and had been responsible for Jethro for four years now. There was a strong emotional bond with the tall lad and she was very worried about him and his future. It had been in her mind that he might be a danger to other children; there had been too many incidents that were out of the ordinary over the past two weeks. But she was struggling to rationalise her fears with the lovely boy that lived with her. She knew the AD and the LADO and nodded a greeting.

The three of them were relaxed with each other and a strong bond that developed arising from the countless meetings that had happened over the years. Jethro's true identity was a deep secret and even the virtual school was unaware.

'I had a late phone call from Sam Perkins, it was just so strange and I wondered if he knew?'

Jennifer shook her head violently and reassured both of them that Mr Perkins, as temporary Head of the virtual school had been under pressure to gather statistics about all of the 'Looked-After Children', or LAC students as they were called. The idea of having one central bureaucratic centre that would check and monitor any child in care had been a good idea at the time but West County had been forced to make severe monetary cuts recently, and this initiative was one of the strong candidates to be stopped.

'Good,' said the LADO, 'I'm convinced that things are slipping out of control and he needs to pull his finger out. But I think his call was just a coincidence.'

'Humph, well, let's have a chat with the boy himself shall we worry about Sam Perkins later?'

The three of them had to walk across the quadrangle next to the MUGA and were clearly visible from the boys' changing room: a purpose-built building that sat outside the main school and next to the MUGA. Jethro caught sight of them and knew something was up, that there would be another meeting, more questions. His relaxed state from the football had dissipated immediately and he felt the primeval urge flood through this system. The 'flight or fight' option was always easy for him. he chose flight each and every time.

~

'Hey Bro, BRO!' Rab saw the long legs of Pencil take him off, round the side of the school and could hear his friend running hard and fast. Rab looked round and wondered what had caused this sudden flight. Then he saw the three adults going into the front entrance of the school.

Behind them he spotted the small figure of Mrs Brooks crossing the quadrangle too. He realised she and his mum would be having a meeting about him. He stood still for just a moment and considered his options. He wanted a fight, he wanted that physical contact with someone, someone who would stop him. But, he also wanted to go and meet Maria, somehow. Not knowing the best course of action he turned and ran round the corner, trying to see where Jethro had gone.

~

Big Tim settled down into the comfortable chair and could feel his muscles soften and relax. There was free coffee in the dentist's waiting room and he was on his second one already. His quick and nimble thumbs were working his phone and he was soon surfing the next diet that he hoped to follow. After all, my body is my temple, he thought to himself.

Maria was in the dentist's chair and the metal clamps were holding her mouth far apart. Carole was lightly touching her hand but that wasn't good enough. The flashbacks for the little girl were proving too much and she had counted to hundred as directed, now she needed the man to stop. She raised a thin arm to show that she needed a break.

IF YOU FAIL TO DREAM. ALL YOU HAVE LEFT ARE NIGHT...

'Just rinse for me will you.' The dentist was a tall man with a large domed head and the spotlight had been bouncing off his bald patch. Maria struggled to rinse effectively with her mouth fixed open and she cast a reproachful look at Carole.

'Just a few more minutes young lady,' the dentist said jovially and gestured for her to return to her position. Another twenty minutes passed and then he gently removed the large pads and other materials from her mouth.

'There, that's tidied things up, but you will need much more work I'm afraid, particularly at the front.'

Maria tried to speak and found that her mouth was so swollen and numb that nothing was understood.

'Yes, try not to speak for a while and definitely no eating.' The dentist looked meaningfully at the care worker.

'No eating for at least five or six hours.'

Carole nodded and gave Maria's hand a reassuring squeeze. She felt for the girl and was only too aware of how hard her brief life had been. The visit out of Hilldowne was only a short respite from her time at the Unit and the treatment could only have been completed at the dental surgery. Maria was a girl who was in danger. More danger than she realised. The risk assessment had detailed the control measures and the peril section had specified that some evil and unscrupulous men were searching for her. It had been the Home Secretary himself as well as Crown Prosecution Service that had decided that she be put in a secure home in Sussex rather than back in Northumbria, for her own protection. It was hoped that her evidence would put a gang of men away for a very long time. However, they were looking for her to make sure that she didn't testify.

SIMON THORPE

The deputy Head wasn't comfortable at all. She shuffled in her chair and prayed that the meeting would end soon. It certainly hadn't started well.

'Mrs Jerome, Mrs Jerome, I'm sure they will bring Rab along very soon. Shall I pop along and check?'

'No, no I'm sure he'll turn up, or I could go?' The social worker didn't want to be alone with Rab's mother either and would have been happy to have left too.

The look of sheer venom both the women got from Mrs Jerome was more powerful than the string of expletives she had been issuing just moments before. She felt that it was the school's and Social Service's fault for everything. She had tried to list the complaints but had lapsed into mere aggression. She felt powerful at the school as she knew that they could be bullied, well, this deputy could anyway. But, she was worried that Rab hadn't appeared.

She clutched her handbag firmly and toyed with the idea of going to the toilet, just a little bit more would help her and, perhaps, the Blokes wouldn't notice? She had spoken to her sister in the taxi and they had decided that the stuff would just be given back to Eric and, perhaps, they would just leave the sisters and their sons alone?

'I need to powder my nose,' she announced as she stood up, and then laughed at her own joke. Both the deputy and the social worker stood up too, grateful for the reprieve and a chance to talk alone.

'Pen, Pen, what is it? What gives bro?'

Rab had followed his friend as quickly as he could and had been surprised to see Jethro jump up and over the wooden fence that surrounded the outdoor swimming pool.

Rab had followed suit and stood with his hands on his hips panting just by the edge of the covered water. The football and the run had shattered him and he knew that he had been smoking too much. His anger at his mother had gone, as quickly as it had come. He was just in the moment.

Jethro was shaking and had started to pace up and down.

'I never hurt her, not me, not me.'

Rab looked up and remembered what he had heard last night.

'Bro, is you dreaming or summat? You was saying that last night,' the teenager moved towards Jethro who instinctively flinched.

'Bro, relax man, I ain't no police.'

'Police, why say police?' Jethro became even more animated and his face started to contort.

'Bro, that's just my word innit, bro, take a chill pill, you's wearing me out.'

Rab held up his arms in a way he hoped would convey his peaceful intentions. But his curiosity was piqued.

'You got a girlfriend Pen? You got something nice to go home to?'

Rab couldn't help himself but leer at the thought.

'No, no, you don't understand, she was my sister, but – I never hurt her, no never.'

Rab looked closely at his friend and gently out his arm round the shaking shoulders of the tall boy.

'Pen, you ain't never hurt anyone, I knows that, we all knows that.'

Jethro suddenly clutched at Rab and the tears flowed, Rab awkwardly held onto the tall boy. Not knowing what else he could do.

∼

'He just took off, and Rab followed him.'

Fi was matter of fact about the two boys shooting off suddenly and was quite bewildered at the reaction from Little Jo and the Head of Care.

'Right, I'll go after them. Fi – go and let Mr Carlyle know, no, Little Jo, you go.'

And with that flourish of real anxiety, she was left alone.

Hmm, she thought to herself, I bet they are only having a cigarette.

But Little Jo had rushed off already leaving her young colleague with far too many boys to monitor. She quickened her step and arrived outside the conference room door, tentatively knocking, she waited for a reply.

∼

Jethro had tried to explain everything to Rab but it was all indecipherable to his friend. Then words were jumbled together and Rab was unaware of any context.

'Bro, just stay here innit, stay here for a while, it's cool here.'

Rab's solution to so many problems was just to ignore them. His philosophy in life was to let things happen and there had been far too much occurring in the past week for him to take on anyone else's issues. Brightening suddenly, he had an idea.

'Listen, just stay here and I'll bring you something you'll like, honest, it's really cool, but later man, later.'

Jethro looked wretched and tried to listen to Rab. Having something from Rab's stash sounded like a golden opportunity and he nodded.

Rab gave a grin and helped the boy hide in the corner of the enclosed area. The pool was only three lines wide and about twenty metres long. It was rarely used except for six weeks each summer, for the rest of the time it was padlocked and covered. He would be safe here.

Rab clumsily climbed over the fence and almost fell on top of H.

'Man, watch out.'

H started to talk immediately, his words rushing out and most of it was nonsense to Rab's mind. But the gist of it was that lots of people were looking for him, that he was in big trouble. Rab looked nonplussed, being in trouble was pretty much a constant with him.

Winking at his friend he said, 'bro, I got to go, you don't say to no one you saw me.'

H nodded quickly, what Rab said happened, that was always the wisest move.

Rab hurried away, skirting round the other side of the school, several boys saw him and he merely gave acknowledging waves, there were very few staff around he noticed. Burrowing in the bushes he retrieved his plastic bag. Making sure that no one saw him. He darted down a small cut-way that led through the undergrowth and, eventually, to the road. It led to the Old Pilot.

14
THURSDAY 11.00 AM 24/11/2018

'The best way of keeping a secret is to pretend there isn't one' —
Margaret Atwood

She squeezed through the small gap easily. Her head was a little woozy but it was her mouth that was totally numb and her tongue felt far too big; she tried to test out the edge of her teeth but couldn't feel anything.

She balanced on the narrow window ledge and dropped quietly to the ground, half landing on a discarded and battered cardboard box. Maria looked around and saw that she was in a narrow passageway. She made her way to the end and stepped out into the sunlight.

The screech of brakes and squeal of tyres sounded far worse than it was, nonetheless, she felt herself get struck and travelled through the air, landing against the black bags of clothes that had been left outside a charity shop.

'My God, oh my God, are you alright?' Maria was half raised and the woman's arms engulfed her. There was a strong smell of flowers emanating from her and a small chain seemed to have swung forward and tapped the girl on her chin.

'Where did you come from? Didn't you look? Oh My God, do I need to call an ambulance?'

The woman was becoming hysterical and her embrace was hurting more than Maria's hip which had caught the impetus of the collision.

Maria tried to speak and knew that her words were incomprehensible. She could see the car parked haphazardly across the pavement and realised she had to stop the woman from attracting too much attention. Her hands tapped at the woman's arms, urgently and constantly, until the grasp was gently released. Maria then stood up and pulled her jumper down. She was wearing jeans and trainers, but her coat was still with Big Tim for safe keeping. She looked at the old woman and gave a clear 'thumbs up' sign. But, forgetting where she had just been, also gave a wide smile.

'Oh my God, your teeth, your teeth! What have I done?'

Maria shook her head and tried to talk again. This time some of the words came out better. Certainly the words 'dentist' and 'treatment' were clearer. Maria was getting anxious now and knew that her absence would be noticed very soon. She had asked to go to the toilet and the window being open was too good an opportunity to miss. Realising her coat and small rucksack would be sacrificed, she had made the decision to go and see Rab and the Griffins. She knew that this adventure would end soon enough and was unaware of the time. But she wanted to do something for herself for a change.

Seeing that the old lady was calming somewhat but still clearly dazed, Maria gave her a small wave goodbye and was about to dash off. But, a passing pedestrian had stopped too.

'Have you hit that little girl?' The middle-aged man was rooting around in his jacket and finally produced an iPhone. Both the old woman and Maria knew that he was about to film and photograph the scene.

Maria put her arms up and covered her face, she moved away and accidentally caught the driver's door which had been left open.

'Quick, let me give you a lift at least?'

In a blur of motion the girl jumped into the car and the woman sat behind the driving wheel. The car started up noisily and, with the exhaust gushing fumes, it drove away leaving the man still fumbling with his phone. She drove for half a mile and pulled up at the end of the high street. The whole thing had only lasted two minutes.

∼

'Tim, TIM! She's not here, check the reception area NOW!' Carole was frantic and she clutched her phone. Should she ring Hilldowne or carry on searching, she really didn't know. Tim sprung from his chair and hurried away.

'Christ, this is not my fault, not me.' His self-preservation thoughts dominated his mind as he came back to Carole and merely shook his head. The two of them dashed outside and traced around the entrance and down the narrow passageway. The small window was still open and it was clear what had happened. Both the care workers were beside themselves and Carole started shouting out Maria's name.

'You two looking for a little girl?' The man had finally managed to hold his phone upright and had been thinking about calling the police.

～

Rab wandered down to the cafe, he knew that the bus stop was just outside it and he was sure that he could get to Hailsham from there. He rarely caught buses and was unaware of when they might run, but his mind was full of his friend Pencil. But he had the confidence of youth on his side. Leaving his mother and the social worker back at the school made him smile.

Sod the lot of them, he thought to himself and glanced up at the sign as it swung back and forth in the sharp November wind. He wondered about the man shown, the 'Old Pilot' and why he only had one arm.

Must have been difficult to fly he mused.

But, he stopped short as the recognisable BMW pulled up and into the two berth car port. Rab quickly ducked behind one of the tall dustbins and his hands were trembling as he pulled his bag close to his chest.

Eric moved his bulk out of the passenger side, his large arms showing through his tight jacket. Another shorter man came out of the driver's side. He was dressed in a smart leather coat, his sunglasses making him look sinister in the murky winter light.

The two men confidently walked into the cafe.

What on earth are the Blokes doing here, Rab thought to himself. He knew that he could not go to the bus stop as he might be seen and he was frozen with indecision.

Just then another car pulled up. This one was an old, battered Escort and the driver was immediately recognisable to Rab too. It was Mrs Arnold. She hurried round to the passenger side and helped Maria out. Rab was transfixed and utterly bewildered. He watched the two of them go into the cafe too. Maria appeared quite happy and was actually holding the old woman's hand. Rab knew that he had to find out about all of this. He wasn't due to meet Maria for another hour, yet here she was. He spotted the way round to the back door and slowly and cautiously edged towards it.

∽

'Yes, she's extremely vulnerable and, yes, yes, and she's been kidnapped, yes, I know, I know.'

Mr Martin had struggled to believe what Carole had told him, and had told her to repeat it back, but really slowly. He had turned on the conference recording device so that he could replay it back to himself once she had finished. The phone call to the police was only the first of several rather difficult conversations he would be having over the next hour or so.

Pausing briefly he pulled out the whisky and genuinely contemplated pouring himself something just to cope with the nagging headache that was threatening to explode into a full migraine. With a hand that was far from steady he rang the AD and was told that she was at a meeting at St Thomas's. he then redialled and rang the school.

Within the space of fifteen minutes two police cars had been dispatched to Hailsham. Big Tim and Carole stayed close to the dental surgery and peered down the road, forlornly hoping that Maria would appear.

'But why would she escape like that, was it planned do you think?'

The large man shrugged his powerful shoulders, he had looked inside Maria's small rucksack and had seen the change of underwear and money but couldn't understand why they would have been left behind. The pedestrian had gone, having missed the opportunity to take the photo he had lost enthusiasm for the whole debacle.

∼

Mrs Arnold had stopped the car and tried to talk to the little girl but Maria was still struggling to make sense due to her numb tongue and was at a loss as what to do next. She had no idea exactly where she was and was regretting the decision to have climbed out of the small window at all. Then she noticed the small pendant hanging around the old woman's neck and she remembered that it had been knocking on her chin just a few minutes ago. It seemed that the small gold griffin had been talking to her.

The old woman was also full of indecision. She had no insurance nor an MOT for the car and had panicked when she had seen the man trying to photograph her. The urge to flee had just taken over. But she knew she could not leave the girl stranded. She wished that she could understand her, but the blurred words coupled with the Northern accent had made it almost impossible to grasp what she was saying at all. Then she noticed the girl studying her locket.

She reached behind her neck and unhooked it, holding it loosely she handed it to the little girl who took it almost reverently.

'It's meant to remind me of my family history, my son bought it for me a long time ago, he's besotted with who the Griffins had once been, he feels we have lost our birthright to power.'

She gave a wan smile as she looked at the girl who was toying with the chain and had held the gold griffin up close to her eye.

'Yes, it's beautiful isn't it, very precious to me,'

She reached across and took the pendant back.

'Yes, I've kept it but not anything else from him.'

She spoke almost absentmindedly as she put the chain back around her head. The little girl was staring at her intently and seemed to pose a question merely with her large eyes.

'Yes, I don't see my son now, well, not for some time, hmm, I think I need to take you to a hospital to be checked over.'

The girl looked horrified and started to speak again, but it was still really hard to make out the words clearly. Suddenly Maria noticed the clock on the dashboard. It said 11.45. She was meant to meet Rab at 12.30 at the large Town Hall. She started to speak again.

This time Mrs Arnold heard some key words, Rab, being one of them. Mrs Arnold relaxed and told the girl that she knew where he was and that her daughter worked at his school. Maria slowly learnt that Jenny was the old woman's daughter. She kept very quiet then as she didn't want anyone to know she had come from Hilldowne, not yet anyway. The two of them set off for The Old Pilot.

∼

SIMON THORPE

The AD took the phone call in the Head's office. She listened and felt her blood boil with anger but this was soon replaced with the icy grasp of fear. Maria being taken was really serious and Jennifer also had a number of phone calls to make. She had absorbed all that Mr Martin had to say and told him she would come over to Hilldowne straight away, she was only five miles away. She then flicked through her address book and found the number she needed.

'Yes, Sam, hi, It's Jenny, now listen.' She quickly outlined the main facts and told the press officer to meet her at Hilldowne too.

If this gets out to the media without careful management my neck is on the line, she thought to herself and made her way towards the main office.

'Where is he, what has 'appened? You lot are useless.'

A thin woman with poorly matching clothes was shouting and waving her arms about, next to her was another woman with dishevelled hair who looked confused and clutched at a battered briefcase. The school's deputy was there too. She too looked out of her depth. Tutting with exasperation Jenny knew that this whole situation was going to explode at any moment. But, she had more important things to attend to.

She stopped to try and get past them when Mr Sinclair shouted out 'Jenny, Jenny, MRS JONES!'

She turned and gestured for the LADO to go into the Learning Resource Room which was situated opposite the small school office. She quickly pulled the door closed on the two of them.

'I've just sent a note to you, I've got to go, can you chair the rest of the meeting?'

'That's just the problem, Jethro has run off, and no one knows where he is.' Mr Sinclair looked uncomfortable and was clearly unnerved by the raised voice of the woman who was still shouting just across the corridor.

The assistant director swore softly to herself and wondered if the day could get any worse. She quickly brought the LADO into her confidence about Maria, he knew she had been at Hilldowne. The two of them were both silently hoping the other would speak up with a solution when Mr Carlyle opened the door.

'Well this is a pickle,' he uttered in his own imitable way. Whenever the pressure was really on he always sought to alleviate it with some gallows humour. But then, he only knew about Rab and Jethro, his eyes widened with real anxiety when they told him about Maria.

~

'Hello Mum, you are looking well, and who do we have here?'

The shorter man had taken off his dark glasses and gave a smile that betrayed very little, his eyes remained as hard as glass. Maria had practically skipped into the cafe and was already planning what she would say to Rab. Seeing this man and a huge scary looking chap standing next to the counter made her wince with trepidation. She clutched onto Mrs Arnolds hand even tighter.

'Jim, Jim...'

The old woman faltered and looked around the cafe but the two men were the only ones there.

'Why are you here, what's going on?'

'Mum, is that any way to speak to your long-lost son? You know Jenny does talk to me and I hear you might have a little bit of a cash flow issue.' He had helped himself to a cup of instant coffee and made a face as he sipped from a white porcelain mug.

Mrs Arnold held the little girl's hand and made her way round the counter and went to the fridge.

'Maria, would you like a drink, something to eat?' She ignored what her son had said and was thinking furiously. She knew that there was an ulterior motive about his visit, but she didn't know what that was, yet.

Maria tried to say 'no' but her mouth was still so numb and she knew she had to say more. She shook her head violently, pointed to her teeth and really concentrating, said, 'I'm not allowed anything for hours yet.'

Jim Arnold was listening intently and said, almost half too himself, 'Is that an accent from up north, hmm, let me see, Newcastle?' He posed the question with a broad thumbs up and Maria instinctively gave him one back. He pulled a phone from his pocket and spoke whilst he was trawling through something on it.

'Ma, Eric has heard that a tart I know is due to see her son at the old school, I just thought I'd see him myself and pop into the Old Pilot to say hi to my old mum at the same time.'

He gave a genuine smile of pleasure as he found what he was looking for, turning the phone sideways and he bent low to show it to the girl.

'Does that look a little like you?' He asked Maria, who gave a squeal of concern and hid behind the old lady's back.

'Hmm, it does, doesn't it, Maria I believe?' He gave his broadest smile yet and added,

'There's some people I know who are looking for you, and here you are, on my doorstep, funny world isn't it?'

'What you on about Jim? Stop it! You are scaring her. What's on that phone? How can you know her?'

The old woman was looking at her apprehensively and knew that something was wrong. Very wrong.

Her son held the phone to his ear and waving his hand grandly, left the cafe, his parting words could be heard.

'Hi, hi, yeah, yeah, it's Jim Arnold, Yeah, the Griffins, yeah, I've got a little package I think you've been looking for?'

Maria and Mrs Arnold held each other and looked at Eric in alarm, his response was to give a big grin and shrug his shoulders.

∽

Rab watched the man leave the cafe, he could hear the phone conversation quite clearly and quickly understood that Maria was in danger. Somehow she had met up with Mrs Arnold and been brought here, seemingly with her agreement, but now this man was negotiating her sale to the very people she was supposed to be safe from. He stood quite still and knew that he had to save her, to get her away from the Old Pilot as soon as possible. But he also knew that Eric was really violent, a very scary man. The other Blokes weren't in sight, Rab didn't know who the smaller man was, but had correctly guessed that he must be the boss. Clutching his bag close, Rab carefully opened the back door and peered inside. He could see the small kitchen that he had stood in just the other night. Sucking his breath in, he entered. Eric could be heard talking and the boy hoped that Maria was safe. Tiptoeing over to the crack in the door, Rab could see that Maria was clutching onto Mrs Arnold, both of them looked very scared.

Eric was eating a bag of crisps and he seemed engrossed in his task. The boy thought that he might be able to push the door slightly open a bit more and catch their attention whilst Eric was busy. But, then Rab had a better idea, softly pushing the doors back he crept towards the end of the office and gently pulled his bag open. He reached inside.

Jim had come back and announced, 'I knew I recognised you, it's little Maria Blake. My, my, you are worth fifty thousand pounds and here you are.'

'Jim, Jim, you are frightening me and this young girl. I thought you had to see some tart or other?'

'Ma, you are right, but that bit of business won't take too long. Actually, I'm more interested in seeing her son Rab.

'RAB!' Both Maria and Mrs Arnold said his name at the same time. The boy gave a startled jump as he heard his name too. He had found the small black gun which had been lurking at the bottom of his bag and he grasped it tightly now. Its grip gave him some comfort and he hoped his fragile plan might work.

~

Jenny Arnold stared at her phone once more. She had read the WhatsApp messages several times but it still made little sense to her. She glanced at the screen and made some simple calculations. If she was quick she should be able to get

IF YOU FAIL TO DREAM. ALL YOU HAVE LEFT ARE NIGHT...

down to the Old Pilot and back in her free session. As the teaching assistants had to work through the lunchtime to help supervise the boys they were all allocated a free session at a different time.

She made her way to the front office and was shocked to see Mrs Jerome being escorted towards a waiting taxi. The deputy and Mr Evans were either side of her and the Head of Care was talking loudly. Asif was already sitting behind the wheel.

'Mrs Jerome, Mrs Jerome, making a scene like this isn't helping.' He quickly pulled the passenger door open and gestured with one wide sweep of his arm that she should get in.

'He's probably just gone for a walk, we will contact everyone and will ring you when he turns up, I promise.'

But Rab's mother was far from being mollified. Her eyes were blazing and she was saying quite a few things under her breath. Jenny Arnold could not make them out. Her heart went out to the mother, who, for all her faults, was still just wanting to know where her son was.

Mr Evans, though, just wanted the vehicle to start up and take this one problem away, just for a while. The disappearance of Jethro was critical and he believed that both boys were together. A search and all the necessary phone calls could be made once Mrs Jerome was off site. Mrs Brooks stood off to one side, watching and listening. How she would later recount this tale was unknown, and something to worry about in a while.

After just a few minutes the car started off down the drive. Jenny had been watching the scene from a vantage point near the MUGA. She now made her way to the front entrance. The deputy Head, Head of Care and the social worker were in a huddle talking. She approached near them and hurried past, going into the school. The receptionist was sitting with her hands on her head, scenes like she had just witnessed we're seriously making her reconsider if she wanted to work at the school.

'Just popping out for about half an hour, I'll sign out.'

Jenny Arnold then half jogged towards the side gate and took the quick route down towards the Old Pilot. As she turned the corner she could see both her grandmother's and father's cars parked in the two bays. She hurried through the front door which had a closed sign up. Inside, she saw a very strange sight.

'Maria, what are you doing here? Are you allowed here?'

Her father turned suddenly and barked out, more in surprise than anger, 'I sent you a text, I was just coming up to the school.' He tried to peer beyond her.

'Is the boy outside then?'

Jenny turned to her father, confusion written across her face.

'Dad, I know what you wrote, but I'm not about to try and entice a boy out to meet a man he has never met in a car park. What's this all about?'

Maria had recognised the care worker and had heard her address the man as father. She understood that this was one family here, but she didn't understand what Rab had to do with it and was terrified about the nasty men that might be coming to take her away. She scanned the room and tried to see a way out. Mrs Arnold was still holding her hand tightly as she, her son and granddaughter started to speak at once. Their voices grew louder and angrier as each refused to listen to the other.

Just then Rab opened the door and threw a bag of white powder into the air. He shouted out and everyone turned to look at him. The powder filled the air and covered the plastic tables and chairs with a smattering of white.

'Here it is, that's what you lot want, take it.' Rab was bellowing and waved a gun around in his left hand.

'Quick Maria RUN!'

Maria shook off the old woman's hand and ran towards him. Both fled through the kitchen and were out onto the road within seconds. Rab reached down and grabbed her hand, half hauling her along.

'What's the blazes, the little runt is really stupid if he thinks that'll work.'

Jim Arnold screamed at Eric, 'get after them its only flour from the kitchen and a toy gun for Christ's sake.'

Eric reacted to his boss's shouting after them and, for a large man, ran very quickly indeed.

Mrs Arnold looked at her son and granddaughter and just sat down, putting her head in her hands.

'Dad, what have you got into? What on earth is going on?'

Jim merely put his finger to his lips and turned to run after Eric.

15
THURSDAY AFTERNOON 24/11/2018

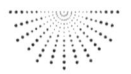

'Griffins, animals that are half eagle and half lion, represented wisdom, strength, and cunning in Greek mythology. They were also believed to hoard and protect gold.' — **Online lesson on Mythology OU**

Jethro could hear them shouting out his name. The distinctive tones of the headteacher and Head of Care resonated through the air and seemed to penetrate straight through him. He huddled closer down in the corner, by the pool, and could feel the memories flood through him. A feeling of being transported back in time seemed to overwhelm him.

'Peter, Peter you rascal, where are you?'

The little boy scooped up his little sister and put his hand over her mouth to stop her calling out. The thin little boy ran with surprising speed out into the garden and, clutching his three-year-old sister tighter and tighter, made his way to perceived safety by the small garden pond. Its crumbly brickwork is just high enough to offer cover.

Jethro fought against the strong memories. He always managed to freeze the image at that point. He knew he must once more. The veil of darkness beyond that point, if drawn back, might spiral him into madness. The teenager stood up, casting aside the memory of the little six-year-old lad.

'I'm Jethro now, Jethro,' he said to himself. Looking around him, he started as he saw the swimming pool. He knew that he could not be near water, not now.

With a massive jump and an athleticism borne out of need rather than natural ability, he cleared the fence and ran. His long legs gathered pace and purpose. He ran, because when he ran he could not think.

'Jethro, Jethro!'

'There he is, stop him!'

Owen Evans was a very fit man, but, at the age of sixty, he knew that his chances of catching the thin boy were negligible. All he could do was watch the boy sprint off down the drive.

∽

'Stop, stop here! Stop, I need to get out, NOW!'

Rab's mother knew that going home would solve nothing. That she had nothing at home to go to either. Her son was everything to her. He always had been. Not having him at home for the past few days had affected her more than she would ever have realised. Rab drove her to distraction each and every day but she also knew that she had been a very poor excuse of a mother to him. She just couldn't go back to the flats, to the misery that was there, she needed time to think.

'JUST STOP THE CAR!'

Asif put the brakes on and pulled up a hundred metres short of the building just at the end of the drive. He was used to passengers behaving strangely and had made it a golden rule to comply with their requests, no matter how strange. His principle of life was to keep his head low. He stayed in his seat and watched the woman in his mirror. She struggled with the seat belt in her anger and irritation but eventually managed to disentangle herself and eased herself out of the taxi.

'I'm going over there for a fag, let me have five minutes, OK?'

Mrs Jerome tottered off towards the converted barn that she knew Rab had been in isolation once or twice. She could see that it was having yet more work done on it. She delved into her handbag and retrieved both her phone and a packet of cigarettes. Forlornly, she scanned the screen.

∼

Rab tugged Maria off the small path that led back to the school and the children ducked under a branch. He beckoned towards a building that could be seen about five hundred meters away and half pushed Maria up a short incline. They made a good two hundred metres before he pulled her behind one of the larger trees. Both were panting as they crouched down. Maria pushed herself into Rab's chest and he put his arms around her. Both the children clutched onto each other and felt a comfort with each other that neither had experienced with anyone else for some time.

Maria felt safe with Rab, she knew that he would do her no harm and that he made her feel special and wanted. She started to softly cry, not with fear, but because she didn't recognise the emotions she was feeling.

'Hey, no crying girl, no crying, I is goin' to sort this.' Rab, too, was feeling emotional, his fear of the Blokes was being overridden by his desire to protect the girl in his arms. She was making him feel important, he felt that he mattered to someone. The pride of that emotion coursed through his veins and with it he felt power. He felt strong.

The two children huddled together, their indecision helped them remain undetected for a few crucial minutes.

~

Jenny Arnold glanced at her grandmother and moved quickly. She hurried over to the old woman.

'Nan, I've no idea what's happening here, but none of it is good. Maria should be at Hilldowne, here, take my phone and ring them, please, just ring.'

The young woman's fingers flew over the small electronic keyboard and she pushed her phone into the woman's hand.

'Nan, he is your son and my father, but he's rotten. A nasty man! Please, ring the police after … promise?'

Jenny didn't wait for an answer but turned and ran out of the cafe and tried to see where the two men had gone. No one was in sight, but she ran up towards the path that headed for the school anyway.

As she ran she lost her battle to stop the tears that poured down her face. She had kept in touch with her father over the years, but at a distance. In her heart of hearts she had known that he was a career criminal. His easy smile and generosity had never disguised the fact to her. But, to be involved with Rab and Maria, like this? As she ran, she made a decision. One that she should have made long ago.

∼

Eric lost sight of the children in the small clump of trees just before the end of the drive. He stopped and peered through the November light. It was moving into the afternoon and the thick cloud cover promised a dark evening. Jim Arnold ran up next to him.

'Can you see them? Where did they go?'

'Don't know, they were over there, then they vanished, must be up at the building.' He pointed, 'Up there.'

Jim nodded and thought through his choices. He didn't like the idea of chasing children around and especially not so close to the school. But, the money that Maria was worth to the people up in Newcastle was mouthwatering. He knew that he could easily get more than the fifty thousand stated on the Dark Web. Additionally, he felt that Rab had to get what was owed to him. The stunt with the flour and the toy gun could make him look ridiculous if word got round.

'Eric, you go up to the building, but quietly. Don't speak to anyone and ring me if you see them, I'll go through this pathway, here.'

Jim Arnold bent low and traced his way through a passageway that he had explored as a boy, he went quietly.

∼

The police car changed direction as soon as the radio announced the new developments. The vehicle described by the pedestrian had shown the owner to be a Mrs Arnold and they were sent to speak to her, they knew the journey wouldn't take too long. The Old Pilot was only four miles away.

'Should we put the siren on?' Asked the driver.

Without waiting for an answer her colleague had switched the button. Both of them liked the opportunity and they sped away.

∼

Mr Sinclair, the AD, the headteacher and the Head of Care were all now aware of the direction Jethro was taking and they all hurried along the drive. The foster mother stayed by the front entrance, the four were holding their phones in their hands, but none of them knew who they should ring or whether it would do any good.

Jenny, the assistant director, heard a ping on hers and glanced down. The media liaison officer was just parking at Hilldowne.

The LADO walked beside her and said under his breath, 'that boy is dangerous and I think we should let the classroom know.'

She gave a grimace and replied. 'We are the "someone" that should be notified, let's hope that those two can calm him down.' She pointed with her head at the two school staff members who were conferring ahead of them.

'Where's the foster mother?'

'She's back at the school.'

As they were speaking Mr Carlyle was saying 'Owen, if he doesn't leave the school premises, and I don't think he will, we are fine, just nab him and get him to calm down.'

The Head of Care nodded and looked over his shoulder.

'Are those two going to be around? I'd rather not get hold of him if they are.'

The headteacher shook his head, 'nah, they've got a little girl missing too; but remember, we also have Rab somewhere.'

The four of them walked quickly up the drive and stopped at the car park. The AD and the LADO quickly conferred with the two men before getting into her car. It was time to split their forces. The headteacher and Mr Evans sighed with relief.

～

Jenny Arnold appeared at the top of the link passageway and was nearly knocked over by Jethro running past her.

'Pencil, PENCIL! Wait.'

But the tall boy carried on, he appeared to be going up to the building at the end of the drive. It was a converted barn that the farmer had used for over a hundred years and was now an off-shoot classroom. The recent building works had made it look even more derelict than before. St Thomas's tended to put anyone in isolation up there if it was safe. The light was going quite quickly and she glanced up, it was cold enough for snow.

Making a quick decision she set off at a run too, up towards the building. There were tall trees on one side that fell away up an incline and the other had a fence that bordered onto the farm next door. She could hear the sound of a quad bike too. The farmer often used one.

Then she made out the large figure of the man that had been with her father. She couldn't see any of the children.

∼

Rab could hear shouting and made out the voice of Jenny Arnold. She appeared to be shouting at Pencil. The boy slowly stood up and looked around him, one of the trees had been cut down some time ago and Rab felt that it looked hollowed out. He held a finger up to his lips and looked at Maria, and, bending low, following its line until he reached the end, unbelievably, there was a space, possibly big enough for the two of them to hide in. He gestured for Maria to come over to him and they softly crawled in, it was snug, but they could not be seen.

Rab gave her a grin and gave her a gentle squeeze for good measure. Both the children were cold, but it gave them a chance to catch their breath and think. Rab produced the pen torch and lit up their faces. Both of them gave a small giggle and they settled down. But, the sound of the classroom coming was soon very clear.

'Rab, Rab, are you here, can you hear me?'

Jim Arnold was slowly searching though the sparse undergrowth, he was almost on top of the hollowed tree and had a strong sense that they were nearby.

'Rab, come out now and that's it. Quits. Hear me? No debt, no trouble. Your mum and even your auntie will be safe. All good. I just want the girl.'

Rab and Maria froze and listened with a growing dread.

'Just give me the girl and your mum will be safe. But, otherwise, well, you know what will happen. Eric will take a hammer to her face and she won't ever work again.'

Maria started to say something and Rab quickly put his hand over her mouth, his eyes pleaded with her to remain quiet. Then they both felt the wood give way slightly, the man was sitting on the trunk.

'Rab, here's the thing, I think you two are in this 'ere trunk, in fact, I think you are wedged in there so tight! I think I'm sitting on you!'

Jim started to gently laugh and suddenly dropped down so that his eye could see through the small niche in the wood.

'Yep, there you are.'

Rab released Maria and he jabbed out with the small stone claw that he had grabbed from his bag. The edge of the talon caught the man in the cheek, making him screech out in pain.

'You little sod, come 'ere!' He roared out his anger as he clutched at his face and caught hold of the stone key.

'What's this, what is this? He stood straight and stared intently at the small stone image.

~

Jethro stood transfixed outside the door. In his head he was six years old again and it was his uncle chasing him. He looked to one side of the building and saw the water trough on the other side of the fence that separated the school grounds from the farmer's lands. Clumsily he negotiated the barbed wire and crouched down behind it.

'Shh, we will be safe here.' His hands were re-enacting the scene from that had laid dormant in his subconsciousness for so many years. His eyes were wild and the tears were forming in his eyes.

'Pencil, Pencil, are you OK?' Jenny had arrived up at the building too, she couldn't see the boy and she was panting and thoroughly confused. Why was Jethro here and why was he behaving so strangely.

'OY, get off that!'

The sudden arrival of the farmer as he drove up to the trough on his quad bike took Jethro completely by surprise.

'Don't you touch that water you little turd.'

'It wasn't me, No NEVER!'

Jethro saw in his mind's eye his arm holding his sister down, with her head under the water, just for a second so that his uncle wouldn't hear her, just for the briefest moment. How she was in the small pond confused him. But he heard his uncle come up and felt the blow to his head. He now saw the girl splutter to the surface and then the man strike her.

'It wasn't ME! I NEVER HURT HER.' He yelled out partly in rage and partly in fear.

'What are you shouting about, what's wrong with you?' The farmer had got off the bike and was approaching the crouching boy.

'No, don't touch him, leave him.' Jenny Arnold shouted out when she saw what was happening, she ran to the side of the building and started to talk quickly to the farmer, who stopped and listened. They both could see the boy repeatedly going through actions as he kneeled next to the trough.

~

Eric watched in fascinated amazement at the scene as he hid behind one of the trees near the door of the building. keeping low he reached for his phone and quickly sent a text message to his boss. He could not see Rab or the girl but was able to make out the familiar sounds of the police siren. A reply came back quite quickly and he nodded in approval. Looking, he spotted something which allowed a small smile of pleasure to pass over his features. He hadn't noticed the taxi as it pulled up to one side. He quickly sent another message.

~

The headteacher and Head of Care could see the outline of Jenny Arnold and they made their way up to her as quickly as they could. As they got closer they could hear Jethro was repeating the same action over and over again. Both men negotiated the barbed wire and moved towards the boy. The TA joined them.

'Pencil, Pen, It's me, Mr Carlyle, it's OK, honestly , it's OK.' With a gentleness that made a nonsense of his appearance and size the old man gently put his arms around the boy who was mumbling now and no longer shouting.

'What's wrong with him? He's a nutcase!' The farmer was clearly agitated and Mr Evans made a beeline for him and started talking to him with soft undertones too. Jenny couldn't hear a word but knew that if anyone could calm the man down it was the Head of Care. She stood by not knowing what to do, there was no sign of her father or the children and she couldn't yet believe her father was involved with child abduction, although she had known about the drug dealing for years. She saw that she wasn't needed here and turned as if to go.

'Miss Arnold, Jenny, can you help?'

Mr Carlyle had stood upright and had one arm around the boy who had stopped mumbling and was starting to look around him in a bleary and bewildered manner.

'Mr Carlyle, I, I mean, yes, but, I…'

The headteacher was staring at her intently and wondered about her indecision.

'Why are you here?'

His question was delivered in a calm and studied way, in a total opposite to the very definite crisis that he was dealing with and she wondered again at the fortitude of people that worked at the school.

'I'm searching for Rab, Rab and the girl from Hilldowne,' she blurted out, her face blushing as she could not make herself say her father's name.

'I'm alright then, thanks, as soon as Jethro is safe I'll come up here too.'

The man and boy struggled through the now growing gap in the barbed wire quickly followed by Mr Evans who took the other side of the boy.

'They are together? You've seen them?'

The headteacher released Jethro to the care of Owen and turned to face the young member of his staff.

'What do you mean? Please explain.'

He appeared so calm and benign, just as he always had. She took a deep breath and quickly told him as much as she could. Her words came out too quickly and soon became jumbled from explaining the facts and what she had guessed. But he allowed her to finish without interruption. By the time she had said all that she wanted the young boy and the Head of Care were already a good hundred metres down the driveway and on their way back to the school.

～

The police car screeched up outside the Old Pilot and the two constables made their way to the front door. One of them saw the old Volvo and pointed it out to the other. All they knew is that a young girl was missing and in danger. Therefore, they entered the cafe cautiously and slowly.

'Oh, you've arrived, I was going to call you, look 999 is on the dial.'

The old woman held up the mobile phone in her hand and was obviously very distraught.

'Miss Arnold, we've had a report that you might know the whereabouts of a…'

The young constable couldn't finish her sentence before her colleague interrupted.

'And what's all this?' Both of the officers took in the whole scene. The cafe was smothered in flour and a small replica toy gun was on the floor.

'You had better explain what's been happening here.'

The older woman looked at the police and shrugged her shoulders. Her world was totally upside down and she was genuinely lost for words.

∽

Rab and Maria were standing very still indeed. The man in front of them was brandishing a vicious and long knife in their faces. He was talking so quietly that the menace was almost more real than if he had been shouting. All three of them were obscured from the driveway due to the trees and they could hear Mr Evans talking to Jethro but could not see him.

'Right, I've had about enough.' Jim wiped some more blood from the scratch on his cheek. He held the knife, point first, at Maria's face and the look on his face made a convincing argument for the children to do exactly as he told them to.

'Stay very, very quiet.' To emphasise his command he pushed the knife so that it was just touching her nose.

The Head of Care and Jethro soon passed beyond earshot and Jim relaxed a little.

'Where did you get this?' He moved the knife so that it was pointing at Rab now.

'No, you don't understand. When I ask a question, you answer it.'

Rab's eyes were wide with fear but he was happier that the knife was directed more to him now. He had been in fights before, and sometimes there had been weapons, but he was in no doubt that they were in big danger.

'I got it from school, from a safe.'

Jim held up the small stone key like a claw. He looked from one child to the other.

'What this is,' he paused and repeated himself, 'what is this, is, is… the thing I've been looking for over a long, long period of time.' He seemed transfixed with the small stone effigy and his speech had altered.

He had to put the claw in his hand with the knife whilst he attended to his phone, he entered a message and then had to reply. Satisfied that everything was in order he then froze as he heard the police siren.

'What's this? Hmmm, sounds like they are going to the Old Pilot.'

He gestured with his knife and pointed up the path.

'Right you two, follow that path, it'll take you up to the old barn.'

Rab looked at Maria and they turned to lead the way up. After just a hundred metres he tapped Rab on the shoulder and they stopped within sight of the old building.

'Do you know what this is? Eh boy?'

Maria pipped up though, 'It's a talon from a griffin.'

Jim looked surprised and even pleased.

'Well done, well done.' he turned it round in his hand and half stroked the end of the claw.

'I think this is a key, a key to treasure that belongs to my family, to the Griffins.'

16
THURSDAY 2.30PM 24/11/2018

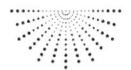

'Nobody owns anything but everyone is rich – for what greater wealth can there be than cheerfulness, peace of mind, and freedom from anxiety— **Thomas More, Utopia**

Jim watched his daughter standing next to an old man in a crumpled suit, they were talking and both clutching their phones. He thought about ringing her but then changed his mind. He didn't like the situation that seemed to be getting worse with each minute. Guessing that the police were interviewing his mother he knew that things were bad. He was holding both children by force and child abduction carried with it some serious prison time. Yet, he believed that the stone key that Rab had found would lead to a long-lost family treasure, and he knew that Maria was worth a fortune.

He sent a text to Eric to meet him by the entrance and made a serious decision. Watching Jenny and the Head suddenly turn and wheel down the drive gave him a chance. As soon as they were out of sight he pushed Rab in the back.

'Right you two, move on, up to the door.'

Reluctantly both children did as they were bid. They were holding hands now and any form of resistance seemed to have vanished. All three were soon standing by the door, the building works by the side had made the site look a mess and part of the exterior wall had been taken down.

Rab squeezed one of Maria's fingers and she looked up at him, he flicked his eyes up and out and she followed the direction he was indicating. There was a gap in the wall and it was being supported by a piece of scaffolding and a buttress. Beyond it was a small area that had the original stonework. The roof had been taken and stored in a classroom. It was that which Rab had wanted to show Maria. But, in this older part of the building, even more Griffins could be seen.

Maria gave a gasp and Jim Arnold turned at the sound.

'What's here, my God! What have we found?'

He lost concentration for a moment as he saw the Griffins too. The exposed cell could only be seen through a small gap and he instinctively moved to look more closely.

Rab, seizing his chance, quickly rooted through his plastic bag and produced the set of keys he had found in the school safe. Fortunately, he chose the right one from the bunch. Rab managed to open the front door, pushing Maria in almost at the same time.

The thrust of the knife took his breath away as he felt it enter his shoulder blade.

'Why you little sod!' Jim had reacted violently and without thought. Pushing the wounded boy aside he went forward and through the door.

'Where are you Maria, come here before I really lose my temper.'

Maria had hidden herself just by a small cupboard and she could hear Rab groaning with pain just outside the door. She heard the man come in and caught a sense of his highly perfumed deodorant. She pushed herself as hard against the wall as she could.

∽

Eric came up to the door and saw his boss stab the boy. Bending low he half picked him up. The boy seemed heavy and the blood from the wound in his back was starting to bleed freely now.

'Are you going to die? I think so.' Eric let the boy go and stood up. His indecision lasted for only a second. Running the fifty metres or so round the corner he saw Asif smoking a cigarette, seemingly oblivious to all that had been curing. Eric couldn't believe his luck.

'Asif, get the taxi started, change of plan, we are leaving, NOW!'

Asif, as ever, keen to follow orders, opened his door and turned the key. Within a minute they had driven off leaving Rab bleeding by the door.

∽

Rab's mother had taken too much, her senses seemed on fire and her whole body was over relaxed. She had been staring at some trees for some time now and her thoughts had fluttered through the years, back to her childhood and the succession of men she had been with, barely any of the memories were good ones. She struggled to think of the dreams she had enjoyed as a girl. The pain of the present seemed to dominate. As though looking though a fog she saw the taxi pass her and, only by concentrating with all her might, did she recognise Eric in the back seat.

'Oy! Come back.' Her voice was merely a croak and she laboriously stood up. She could hear voices, one in particular was familiar, that of Jim Arnold.

∼

'Maria, Maria, come out, I know you are in here, there's no point in hiding, come on out.'

Jim was holding the knife in his left hand and frantically texting Eric with his right. He wanted that taxi now and knew that he and the girl had to leave.

Maria slipped through a small screen and into a bare classroom. The parts of the roof were being stored there and she could see the Griffins had etched parts of it. Opening her eyes wide she crept past the blocks and found the plasterboard was loosened. Wriggling ever so quietly she managed to edge behind it.

'Come on out, I haven't time for this, you know what will happen to you if you don't.' Jim's voice was permeating through the small area as he picked and kicked at the furniture, upending chairs and desks. Then he saw the screen, which had been moved to reveal the small area that seemed to lead to the outer wall. He paused when he saw the blocks with the Griffins and smiled.

'So, this is it, this is where the old nun lived and died.'

IF YOU FAIL TO DREAM. ALL YOU HAVE LEFT ARE NIGHT...

Maria could hear him and was shaking with fear. Her thin and bony body was cold already, but the icy grasp of terror was pervading her every thought.

She thought that he must have killed before and buried someone here, none of it made any sense and she was so scared for Rab. She looked around the crammed space. The old brickwork and lack of light made her feel invisible. All she could see was a darkening of the sky through the gap in the wall. She saw that the snow had just started to fall.

∼

The police had traced their way up the path and radioed back that there was still no sign of the children. But they were able to explain that Maria was with a boy called Rab. They called for backup.

∼

Mr Carlyle and Jenny reached the top of the passageway and almost bumped into the two police constables. It didn't take long for the four of them to realise that they had to go back to the building at the end of the drive. The snow was falling faster now and the Head knew that the school could soon be snowed in, it had happened before. He rang the school and spoke to Big Jo.

'Yes, I know, but it's my decision. Anyone that is still at school needs to be sent home now. That's everyone that should be staying tonight in the Residential. Now, has Owen calmed Jethro down? Yes, that's good. Right, I'm busy now, so, please ring the AD, yes, and tell her.'

He explained what his assistant head had to say. As he was speaking he noticed the taxi drive off.

The police had seen the car too and they broke into a steady jog.

Mrs Jerome almost fell over her son and gave a shriek of alarm as she saw the red of the blood mingling with the white of the snow. She threw herself on him and cradled his head in her hands.

'Rab, Rab, my God, what's happened? Who did this?'

Rab heard his mother through the pain and sheer instinct took over.

'Gerrof ya silly cow.' He half pushed her away with his left arm. His right just wouldn't move. She half stood up and helped him back to his feet.

'Mum, Mum, where's Maria? The Blokes did this!' He felt dizzy and suddenly nauseous.

Mrs Jerome had a type of anger that gripped her that over-rode all other emotions. She looked up and saw a glimpse of Jim through the gap. He looked up at the same time and gave her a ghastly smile.

She ran. Running with a speed that no one expected. She was through the door and into the small space within a matter of seconds. Her hand held her highly heeled boot and she was screaming. But Jim caught her arm easily and almost dismissively struck her with his free hand. The blow made a horrific crunching sound and she fell unconscious immediately. But this had created just enough time for Maria to slip back out of the space. Looking around she saw a discarded hammer. Glancing up she heaved the hammer up as high as she could and brought it down against the scaffolding pole.

'There you are, come here little girl.' Jim had turned and lurched forward but his foot caught the prostrate form of Rab's mother and he fell against the post at the same time as she brought the hammer down. A piece of masonry fell and blocked the space. It missed him but blocked the small space.

∽

The flow of the blood had stopped and Rab slowly bent down to pick up the knife. Each step was like a mile and he had only made a short distance when Maria threw herself into his arms.

'Rab, are you alright, oh, I thought you were dead.'

Rab nearly fell over and tried to hold the girl away.

'I is alright, but stand back, no one hurts you. No one.'

The fire in his eyes betrayed his true emotion. For once he wasn't doing anything too quickly. He had decided to take a life and knew that his decision was a good one. He had to find his mother too.

'Hey, Rab, Rab, come here boy.'

Jim was talking to him through the gap, just his head was visible. He pushed an arm out and gestured to the children.

'Help me out and everything will be OK. Just come here.'

His voice was full of gentle coaxing yet still carried an implied threat.

'Where's my mum?' Rab was struggling to stand upright, the pain was almost all consuming. Maria held him tightly with one small arm.

'How did you get that?' Jim was screaming now.

Maria looked down and was shocked to see that she had the claw in her hand. She must have picked it up but had no memory of doing that.

∽

Two hours later the two colleagues were sitting in the Head's office. The snow was falling very heavily and both of them knew that they would be snowed in. It had happened before and they weren't too worried, there was food aplenty.

'Well, that was a strange day.'

Mr Evans gave a wan smile, as ever, the headteacher was taking everything in his stride.

'So, what will happen, well, to everyone?'

Mr Carlyle slipped back into his swivel chair, whilst he was able to project a calmness, he knew that he could not take many more days like this. Perhaps it was time to take his pension.

'Jethro won't come back, my guess is that his name will be changed again and that he'll be moved to another part of the county.'

'So, do you think he did kill his sister?'

The head ruminated for a time and nodded.

'Yes, I know it's hard to accept, but those actions he kept repeating, yes, I think he did.'

Both men stopped and paused, the boy that they had known for three years, was he really capable of such a thing? Both of them took a sip of their hot drink.

'And Maria?'

The headteacher gave a grim smile.

'That's an easy one, she will go to another secure unit, where she will be safe.'

'And the people looking for her?'

Both men knew the answer to that, they may be caught, but then again, they may not. It depended on how much Jim Arnold would say, whether he would help 'the police with their enquiries.'

The past two hours had been absolutely manic for the two of them. The snow had hindered everything, but the police had managed to move the masonry enough to get in and arrest Jim. He had been shouting about his birthright, but nothing he said had made sense to the officers. Rab and his mother had been sent to hospital and Social Services were now heavily involved. The assistant director and her media liaison officer had worked some kind of miracle and the press just didn't know that anything had happened. The only relic of the events were some cones making the building at the end of the drive secure.

'So, can I see it again?' Mr Evans knew that the stone box was just hidden under the Head's desk.

Mr Carlyle nodded his assent and retrieved it. The damage up at the building had dislodged it sufficiently for it to be seen. It had been Maria that had put the key in and opened it whilst they had waited for the ambulance. Both Rab and his mother had lost consciousness and Jenny Arnold had been adept in keeping them both warm and comfortable. It had been relatively easy for Mr Carlyle to casually put his coat over the box and bring it back to school.

The two men stood by his desk and reviewed it once more. It was tiny, half the size of a shoe box. The locking mechanism had broken as soon as Maria had put the claw in. It was empty except for three gold objects.

'Do you think Rab will come back here, to the school I mean?'

The head gently took out the two pieces of shaped gold, when placed together they clearly made a gold griffin, it was evident that they had been made that way, to interlock or to be kept separately. He held one up to his eye and scrutinised it. The other he passed to his friend, who had to grapple with finding his glasses before. He, too, scanned it.

'Yes, I think so, I hope so anyway.'

The Head carefully put the intricate gold talon down.

'This is where he belongs, this is where he should be.'

'But surely he will be taken from his mother surely?' Mr Evans persisted with his questions. His bushy eyebrows were furrowed with the effort of making out the small body of the lion. Both men knew that whilst the craftsmanship was quite poor, but that it was unique.

'Of that there is no doubt, he will go into care.' The head-teacher brought out the thin gold ring, it was far too small to fit either of the two men's large fingers. It had been made for a young woman a long time ago.

'Yes, I think Mrs Jerome may spend some time in prison, that was a lot of cocaine they found in her handbag.

The two men felt old and suddenly tired. Nearly all of the decisions they had been talking about were to be taken by others rather than themselves. Then they looked at each other.

'Well?' It was the headteacher's turn to ask a question.

'What do you think, should we do it?'

Mr Evans considered the proposal for a second time. He knew that his compliance was critical, no one else knew about the contents of the box. Even Maria hadn't seen inside.

'Yes, yes, I think it's fine.'

'Sure? It's a strange one, but I think it's right.'

They both knew that it was time for them to retire, that a secret like this would make working together impossible in future. But, it was time.

∼

The next morning both men had made themselves a hearty cooked breakfast and looked out at the three floor snow drifts.

'OK, I've written this up, it is fine, I'm sure. It was all found on school property.'

Mr Evans knew that this supposition was a stretch of the imagination. But he was happy with the decision made the previous night.

He watched the head place the ring and the gold griffin in an envelope addressed to Jenny Arnold.

'They are, technically, hers and with her father going to prison, it's a nice gesture.'

'So strange, a woman living most of her life in that small cell and then a descendant actually working here.'

The headteacher shrugged his shoulders.

'Yes, and the connection to his House and the Old Pilot.'

'But.' The old man licked the envelope and placed it on his desk.

'But, how extraordinary that all of this became connected to Rab and Maria.'

'Will the children be alright?' It was a question that the Head of Care asked himself a lot. About all the pupils.

'Yes, I think they will, they are survivors.'

The Head stretched his aching shoulders and the two of them turned to look out at the snow once more.

EPILOGUE

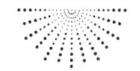

1516

Sir Thomas More carefully undid the bundle. He nodded at the mason who withdrew some way off. The stone box was a little too small but it would suffice. Thomas lay the ring and two parts of the griffin on top of his copy of Utopia, his book. It was wrapped in some oilskin and he hoped it would last the test of time.

Nodding with satisfaction as the box fitted into the space created, he turned the key with a resounding crack. He then pushed the claw into place in the wall.

'Father, I've put the papers in your bag.' A young woman spoke up.

'Thank you daughter, the secrets of the old queen must be taken away. Never to be revealed.'

'What happened to the old lady, the nun?'

'She died a lonely old man woman, that is all you need to know.'

He walked away from the building, its role was now just for storing agricultural produce. Sir Thomas had bought the old Manor House and had installed some tenants. He was glad she was finally dead, that she would have found peace at last. He was pleased to have left her last two treasures and smiled at the thought of his gift of the book. He looked up at the sky and hoped that she would read it, somehow.

'Father, are you crying?' Asked his daughter.

'No, not at all, but just remember, if you fail to dream all that is left are nightmares.'

'didn't she dream then?'

'No, she did not.'

End

Printed in Great Britain
by Amazon